William George Ward

Science, prayer, free will and miracles

An essay

William George Ward

Science, prayer, free will and miracles
An essay

ISBN/EAN: 9783337278786

Printed in Europe, USA, Canada, Australia, Japan

Cover: Foto ©Andreas Hilbeck / pixelio.de

More available books at **www.hansebooks.com**

SCIENCE, PRAYER,

FREE WILL, & MIRACLES.

AN ESSAY,

REPRINTED FROM THE "DUBLIN REVIEW,

OF APRIL, 1867.

BY

WILLIAM GEORGE WARD, D.Ph.

Second Edition.

LONDON:

BURNS & OATES, 17 PORTMAN STREET,

AND 63 PATERNOSTER ROW.

1882.

Price One Shilling.

CONTENTS.

—◦◦—

PREFACE TO THE SECOND EDITION.

MY first edition of this reprint was, from acci-
dental circumstances, an unusually small
one, and my publishers tell me that it is already
sold off. In putting forth a second, I must express
my gratitude for the very favourable and cordial
criticisms which I have received; and I will add a
few remarks, which have been suggested by one of
these criticisms. What little I have to say, will
refer exclusively to the *first* of my three themes; as
my treatment of Free Will and Miracles has not (so
far as I know) elicited any comment whatever.

I have explained throughout, that the position
which I assume is purely negative. Go back some
three hundred years: Christians, I suppose, never
thought of doubting, that (to use Mr. M'Coll's
excellent expression, see p. 37) "God is behind
the veil of Nature, *working always.*" They knew
of course that many phenomena proceed on fixed
laws; but they took for granted that He directs and
uses those laws according to His good pleasure,
from moment to moment. Nothing therefore was, in
their view, more simple and natural, than to pray
God or invoke the Saints for such temporal blessings

as they might desire. In proportion however as inductive science made progress,—in proportion as men came to understand that (not *many* but) *all* phenomena succeed each other according to uniform and invariable sequence,*—an impression seems to have gained ground, that there is some difficulty in the way of supposing that God does thus continuously direct the course of Nature. My purpose in this Essay has been to argue, that no such difficulty exists in the very slightest degree; that the notion of its existence is the merest delusion. As regards indeed belief in God's continuous agency throughout the phenomenal world,—I maintain that the facts of inductive science not only do not render that belief one whit *less* probable, but that they even make it somewhat *more* probable, than it was three hundred years ago.

It has been pointed out however by a Catholic critic, that this theory, as to God's continuously premoving natural laws, is by no means necessary, in order to vindicate that great Christian verity, the efficacy of prayer for temporal blessings. Such prayer, he suggests, was of course (to speak according to human methods of conception) foreseen by God at the time of creation; and it may therefore have had its full influence with Him, when He originally appointed the laws of Nature. Now the doctrine here implied is true beyond all possible question; and

---

* I do not admit of course that this statement is strictly true; because both Free Will and Miracles constitute exceptions to uniformity of phenomenal sequence. But this fact does not bear on my immediate theme.

indeed it is a doctrine, which Christians not very unfrequently reduce to practice. It may well be e.g., that some one very dear to me dies, in regard to whom I should be only too happy to think that he is in Purgatory, however protracted his detention there may be. Lugo somewhere points out that, after his death, it is by no means unmeaning or necessarily unavailing to pray for his salvation; because such prayers were foreseen by God, and may have influenced Him to grant the dying man some special grace at the last.

Here then the question arises, how far it is probable that this is the appointed method, whereby alone (apart from direct miracle) prayer for temporal blessings can avail with God. Of course, probably enough it is *one* method; but is it the *only* or the *chief* method. There are two rival theories in the field,—concerning God's relation to the fixed laws of Nature,—which may be called respectively the " premovement " and the "independence'' theories. According to the former,—God is (as Mr. M'Coll says) " behind the veil, working always " ; He continuously premoves and impels, according to His good pleasure of the moment, those fixed laws of physical sequence, which He established at the period of creation. According to the latter theory,— having once established those laws, He leaves them to operate spontaneously, independently, blindly, without interfering with their movement. Which of these theories should Catholics regard as more probably the true one ? A worthy discussion of this point could not be otherwise than somewhat lengthy. But I will jot down most briefly my own humble opinion thereon, and the reasons by which I should support it; submitting it however, in all sincerity, to the judgment of more competent authorities.

I would ask at starting, for what reason, as a matter of fact, the "independence" theory was first thought of. It is certainly open to great objections. In the first place, as I urge in p. 26, the notion of a Creator self-excluded from interference with the movements of His own work,—is a possible indeed, but to a Christian surely an almost incredible hypothesis. Then further, I cannot but think that this theory would impose a very unnatural sense on many passages of Scripture. Take one out of a thousand instances. "Elias prayed that it should not rain; and it rained not for three years and six months: he prayed again," and the rain came (James v. 17, 18). Does St. James mean to say, that this succession of drought and rain was due exclusively to the laws of Nature established at the Creation? that Elias's prayer had no efficacy whatever, resulting at the time of its utterance? And many similar instances will occur to every one. Or consider the plagues of Egypt. No Christian of course would suggest, that these came in the ordinary and normal course of physical events; but it might be said, no doubt, that they were express *miracles*,—express violations of the laws of Nature. Yet Scripture seems to imply the reverse. "The Lord made a hot wind to blow for the whole day and night; and next morning *the wind* brought the locusts" over all Egypt. Afterwards, "He made a *most strong westerly wind to blow*, and cast the locusts into the Red Sea"

(Exodus x. 13, 19). It would appear then that, on this occasion at least, He did not violate, but premove, the laws of phenomenal sequence. An equally solid objection to the theory which I criticise may be founded (I think) on the consentient view of Christian Antiquity ; but, for brevity's sake, this particular point may be pretermitted. I venture therefore to ask again why, in the teeth of such grave difficulties, the "independence" theory has been started. There can be no second answer to this question. The theory has been invented, because some Christians have thought that the progress of inductive science has made the earlier and traditional view untenable. Were it not for this supposition, no one would have dreamed of the "independence" theory at all. But this supposition is the precise allegation, which I point-blank and emphatically deny in my present Essay. I maintain confidently, not only that the facts of science have failed to make the traditional theory untenable, but that they have made it somewhat more probable than even it was before. Since therefore no Christian would have dreamed of the "independence" theory, had it not been for a supposition which I consider demonstrably unfounded,—I think of course that the said theory is improbable, in a degree which one cannot easily exaggerate. And this would hold, even were there not one further objection to it, which I shall presently mention.

Before going further however, I must notice one particular point which here suggests itself. I fully admit (see p. 26) that there is one conceivable conclusion of physical science, which *would* disprove the " premovement " theory ; though I have argued that the course of science has hitherto been, not *towards* this conclusion, but in the directly opposite direction. An inquirer then may ask, Do I maintain as absolutely *certain*, that scientific researches will never land us in this thesis ? do I stake (as it were) the very truth of Christianity on this scientific issue ? Here again I will most briefly express my own humble opinion ; submitting it however, even more earnestly than before, to the judgment of competent authorities.

Now there is evidently a most close connexion, between God's relation to *physical* and *psychical* phenomena respectively. In the first instance however I will answer the inquiry just now mentioned, as though this connexion did not exist; as though we had to consider no other phenomena, except those of the material world. If this were the case, I do not think we should have ground for absolute *certainty*, that the " independence " theory may not turn out to be the true one. I think indeed that the interests of revealed religion would sustain a heavy blow, if any such conclusion were attained ; but I do not see that the truth of Christianity would be thereby actually disproved.* I do think that the interests of revealed religion would

---

* It can hardly be necessary, I suppose, to make an obvious explanation. If I said that some given scientific thesis would disprove the truth of Christianity,—I should not of course mean that I have the very slightest doubt of Christianity ; but only that I am absolutely certain that no such scientific thesis will ever be proved.

receive a heavy blow, were the "independence" theory scientifically proved; and that, for more reasons than one. I think that Christians would find it far more difficult than they do, to realise God's Omnipresence and pervasive Power; while yet such realisation lies at the very root of practical piety. I think also that their due reverence for Scripture would be greatly impaired, by their having to understand so many texts in a non-natural sense. Lastly, I think that the quality of their prayers, at various crises of their life, would suffer grievous detriment. At the same time, for the reasons I have already given, I rejoice to think that the scientific result here supposed is improbable (as I have said) in a degree which one can hardly exaggerate.

But now let this further fact be carefully considered. Those who, on the ground of inductive science, hold the "independence" theory in regard to *physical* phenomena,—for obvious reasons commonly extend the same theory to *psychical* phenomena also. Psychology is no less truly an inductive science, than is meteorology or chemistry. Now let us see what is involved in this. The Christian prays for strength under temptation, and for growth in virtue. What is meant by such prayer? He supplicates, that actual grace be granted him in a certain special degree, at certain opportune moments. What is an actual grace? It includes primarily the inspiration of a certain thought; * not to mention the infusion

---

* No doubt the thought is supernatural; but it is not on that account the less a thought, a mental phenomenon.

of certain other mental phenomena also. But if the "independence" theory held concerning psychical phenomena,—we should have to infer, that God has bound Himself down never to give any human being any grace, which is not strictly determined beforehand by the laws of the human mind; any grace which an ideally perfect psychologian might not have predicted with certainty before the event. I need not waste words, to impress on Christians how simply intolerable is any such hypothesis.

We may be absolutely certain therefore (I submit) that no scientific argument will ever be discovered, which establishes the " independence " theory as applicable to psychical phenomena. And since it is certainly among the most grotesque of hypotheses, that God premoves indeed psychical phenomena, but leaves physical phenomena alone,*— an additional probability is surely added to the probability which was already enormously great, that, in regard to *physical* phenomena also, the " independence " theory is assuredly a mistaken one.

Since the preceding remarks were sent to press, I have observed a very interesting passage in a letter of Dr. Thirlwall's, the late very distinguished Protestant Bishop of St. David's. I earnestly sympathise with its general drift; though I need hardly explain that I by no means intend to imply agreement with every single one of the writer's propositions. The passage runs thus :—

---

* See also the additional note at p. 33.

The education, of which the Bible is a record, is only the *moral and religious* education [of mankind]. But to this, in later times, and in some sense it may be said in our own day, there has been added a new branch of education,—the scientific,—which, in itself, is perfectly distinct from the other, and not only no part of the religious and moral development, but apparently rather at variance with it; for it has introduced man to the knowledge of a vast system of secondary causes, previously unknown and unsuspected, which seem to separate him from God, and to exclude the idea of the immediate divine presence and agency, which was the condition of his early piety. Whether it really does this, or only seems to do it, is the question of deepest interest to all religious minds. If that system of secondary causes is, as men of science are apt to regard it, an adamantine clockwork, without any provision for continual adaptation to varying circumstances, it is to my thinking of the smallest possible importance whether we admit or deny the being of God. For, at the best, He is now " functus officio," and enjoying an everlasting holiday ; only differing from the Epicurean, in as much as it has been earned by work now done. The great problem of our day seems to me to show, that the childlike belief of man's early days is consistent with the fullest acceptance of all scientific truth, and that there is no reason why this should quench faith or stifle prayer. I think that an important step is gained, when it is shown that science at least does not, and cannot, disprove this, and that it is consistent with all our experience of human action.—(Letters of Connop Thirlwall, edited by Perowne & Stokes, pp. 255, 256.)

I ought further to explain that, when I wrote my article in 1867, I was not acquainted with that particular suggestion for reconciling the efficacy of prayer with the uniformity of nature, which I have been considering in the earlier part of this Preface. Consequently I speak throughout, as though those who advocate the " independence " theory necessarily denied the availableness of prayer for temporal blessings. *Now* of course I entirely retract this implication : which however is so embedded in the structure of my paper, that I could not make the requisite changes without re-writing the whole.

I have a word now to add on quite another subject. In page 29 I asked, " When did the Church ever pray against comets and eclipses ? " implying of course that she *never* did so. A correspondent objects to this statement, because of a fact which occurred under the reign of Callistus III. At that time, says my correspondent, all Europe was in consternation at the appearance of Halley's comet; and the Pope organised prayers, supplicating that, if the comet portended disaster, such disaster might visit the Turks rather than the Christians. I have not cared to verify the details of this statement, because it is so entirely irrelevant. No doubt, an anti-Catholic objection might be built on it from a *different* point of view; though I think that such objection would be very easily met. But as regards my own argument, the fact does not present any even superficially plausible difficulty. I have contented myself therefore, with slightly altering my language; so as to exhibit still more clearly—what the context however was sufficient to show—my real meaning in the question.

I have inserted a very few more additional notes, which (like those added in my first reprint) are within brackets. I have also made a very few little changes in the text.

January 23, 1882.

PREFACE TO THE FIRST REPRINT.

SINCE the following paper was first published, the theme which it treats has received far more prominent attention than had befallen it in the year 1867. Nevertheless I have not happened to observe any Theistic argument, which (as I think) entirely supersedes,—nor yet any Antitheistic argument, which (as I think) tends to invalidate,—my own humble suggestions. I am led to republish them at the present moment, because they are connected with an article of mine, just finished, which is to appear in the "Dublin Review" of next January; and because the "Dublin Review" of April, 1867, is entirely out of print.

My general drift is (I trust) sufficiently obvious. The "uniformity of nature" is a truth, which lies at the very root of inductive science; insomuch that if that uniformity did not exist in a fully sufficient sense, the notion of inductive science would be a dream. Yet it appears on the surface, that to affirm the uniformity of nature, is to deny the existence of Free Will; the existence of miracles; the efficacy of prayer, whether for temporal or

B

spiritual goods. In other words, it appears on the surface, that a certain truth, accepted most firmly by all cultured men without exception, leads by immediate consequence to profoundly irreligious conclusions. The purpose of my article is to show, that what seems on the surface a true inference, is not really a true inference at all. I wish to show, that the Theist may earnestly and confidently believe in Free Will; in miracles; in the temporal and spiritual efficacy of prayer; while nevertheless he shall ascribe to the uniformity of nature a fully sufficient area, for the reasonable construction of inductive science. I concede most cordially, that the conclusions of inductive science are established with entire certainty; but I maintain at the same time, that the above-named religious doctrines may none the less be most assuredly true. I do not profess in the following article to show that they *are* true; but merely that they *may* be true, without inflicting any kind of injury on the foundations of inductive science.

There is one point to which I would invite especial attention. Some Christians (I venture to think) are too ready to admit, that the whole course of physical phenomena has been fixed once for all by Almighty God; and that prayer therefore can have no effect towards changing that course from moment to moment. I have argued, from p. 15 to p. 34, that the interests of inductive science do not in any way demand such an admission. But what I here wish especially to point out is, that whatever argument would suffice to disprove the efficacy of prayer

for temporal goods, must equally disprove its efficacy
in the moral and spiritual order. If prayer for fine
weather were unavailing against God's "irrevocable"
decree,—so equally prayer must be unavailing for
help against temptation, or for growth in virtue.
I have argued this in pp. 6, 12, 36. But there is
really not the very slightest ground for either supposition. Let it be conceded for argument's sake,
that the laws of phenomenal sequence, both psychical
and physical, are universally and irrevocably "fixed."
There would still be no difficulty whatever in the way
of our holding, that the whole phenomenal universe,
of which the laws are thus "fixed," is nevertheless at
every moment "premoved" by its Author at His
pleasure, according to the designs of His Providence
at such moment.

But, although the supposition I have just made
would have no injurious bearing on the efficacy of
prayer, there are two other religious doctrines to
which it would be entirely fatal. If the laws of
psychical sequence were absolutely and irrevocably
fixed, there could be no *Free Will;* and if the laws
of physical sequence were absolutely and irrevocably
fixed, there could be no *Miracles.* I argue however,
from p. 39 to p. 50, that psychology still remains a
genuine inductive science, though the doctrine of
Free Will be ever so unreservedly accepted. And
I argue, from p. 50 to p. 54, that Miracles, however
frequent they may be,—and for my part I believe
that they are extremely frequent,—have not even
the slightest tendency to shake the foundation of
inductive science.

I have made no substantial change whatever in the article ; but have added, within brackets, a very few supplementary notes.

It will be seen that throughout I have been primarily addressing the Catholic inquirer. And on the whole subject,—a subject (I need hardly say) of quite incalculable importance in the Theistic controversy,—I can only repeat here what I say in p. 55 :—

Si quid novisti rectius istis,
Candidus imperti : si non, his utere mecum.

Oct. 28th, 1881.

SCIENCE, PRAYER, FREE WILL, AND MIRACLES.

Five Discourses on Miracles, Prayer, and the Laws of Nature. By REV. D. GILBERT, D.D. London : Farrell.

The Reign of Law. By THE DUKE OF ARGYLL. London : Strahan.

The Church and the World. Essay 16. *Science and Prayer.* By REV. M. M'COLL. London : Longmans.

NOTHING can be clearer, than that God desires mankind to cultivate experimental science. He has imprinted on nature fixed laws, which make it amenable to such science ; and He has endowed man with an intellect capable of investigating those laws. Then such investigation is morally advantageous to many ; is a good intellectual discipline to all ; and has issued moreover in the discovery of innumerable truths, which have promoted physical enjoyment and social comfort in a degree almost incredible. And the Church has ever thus interpreted God's Will. No one can maintain with the slightest plausibility, that, even when her influence was greatest, she occupied any other attitude towards science * than that of respect and encouragement ;

---

* In this article we shall, for convenience sake, use the word "science" in the sense which Englishmen so commonly give to it ; as expressing physical and experimental science, to the exclusion of theological and metaphysical.

still less that she viewed it with misgiving or sus-
picion. And yet, in full consistency with this avowal,
we may and do regard it as a serious evil, that
the great triumphs of science have been achieved at
a time like the present; at a time when (from causes
easily to be traced however deplorable) there has
been so large and wide-spread a rebellion against
the Church's authority over secular thought. It has
resulted from this circumstance, that science and
theology have proceeded for centuries past, each in
its own separate sphere, and each ignoring the
other's existence. On the one hand, scientific men
have continually assumed many a principle fundamentally irreligious, which they have not cared however to express and carry forward into its legitimate
consequences. On the other hand, theologians have
confined themselves to that high sphere which is exclusively their own, without troubling themselves to
consider and correct what has been amiss in humbler
regions of speculation. Such, we say, has been the
state of things for many successive generations.
But at length there are no doubtful signs, that this
chasm between the two different lines of thought is
beginning to be bridged over, and that the tem-
porary truce is to be succeeded by a vigorous war.
Every one has observed how much greater interest
is taken in matters theological—whether the interest
of sympathy or of disgust—than was the case even
twenty years ago. Scientific men are beginning to
attack openly the foundations of religion; and cor-
relatively no duty is at this moment more indis-
pensably urgent on the theological faculty, than to
confront and encounter these malignant and formidable attacks.

Our present purpose is to consider what appears
to us at once the most specious and the most fundamental of all those objections, which have been
brought against religion in the name of science. It
cannot indeed be adequately treated, except in a

volume, or rather in a series of volumes. All which we can hope to accomplish in an article, is to lay down principles in reply, which may recommend themselves both as true and as sufficient; and which may be more fully apprehended and also carried out into due detail, by those Christian thinkers who are adequate to the task.* We shall endeavour to state the objection in its full strength and extent; because nothing can be more injurious to the Church's cause, than that her defenders should fail to apprehend the fatal malignity of that pestilence which is abroad. There are not a few scientific men then, we fear, who (if they spoke out their full mind) would argue as follows:—

" The one principle, implied in every scientific
" investigation of every kind, is the principle of
" *phenomenal uniformity;* or, in other words, the
" principle that, in every case without exception,
" where there are the same phenomenal antecedents,
" the same phenomenal consequents will result.
" Let me suppose for a moment the contradictory
" of this;—let me suppose, e.g., that some deity
" had the power and the will to affect the fixed laws
" of nature;—science would be an impossibility. I
" compose a substance to-day of certain materials,
" and find it by experiment to be combustible: I
" compose another to-morrow of the very same ma-
" terials, united in the very same way and in the
" very same proportions, and I find the composition

---

* The present writer should confess at starting, what will (he fears) be manifest throughout; viz., that he labours under the great disadvantage of complete unacquaintance with all details of physical science. We should add however, that a Protestant gentleman of high scientific eminence has done us the very great favour of looking over our sheets.
[This was the late Professor De Morgan. He gave no opinion (as far as I remember) on the conclusiveness of my argument; but pronounced that I had not fallen into any blunder through my ignorance of physical science.]

" *incombustible.* If such a case were possible, the
" whole foundation of science would be taken from
" under my feet. Science from the first has assumed
" this phenomenal uniformity, as its first princi-
" ple; nor could it have advanced one single step
" without that assumption. Those achievements
" then of physical science, which the most religious
" men cannot attempt to question, afford an abso-
" lutely irrefragable demonstration of that first
" principle which science has from the first assumed.
" No investigations, proceeding throughout on a
" false basis, could by possibility have issued in an
" innumerable multitude of unexpected yet experi-
" mentally true conclusions.

" But now answer me candidly : how is this prin-
" ciple of phenomenal uniformity reconcilable—I
" will not say with Christianity—but with any prac-
" tical system whatever of religion ? I will begin
" with my weakest point of attack, and rise by de-
" grees to my strongest. I will begin with the
" doctrine, that prayer for temporal blessings is
" reasonable and may be efficacious. Your country
" is visited with famine or pestilence ; and you suppli-
" cate your God for relief. Your only child lies
" sick of a dangerous fever ; and as a matter of
" course you are frequent in prayer. You are dili-
" gent indeed in giving her all the external help
" you can ; but your chief trust is avowedly in God.
" You entreat Him, that He will arrest the malady
" and spare her precious life. What can be more
" irrational than this ? Would you pray then for
" a long day in December ? Would you pray that
" in June the sun shall set at six o'clock ? Yet
" surely the laws of fever are no less absolutely
" fixed than those of sunset ; and were the case
" otherwise, no science of medicine could by possi-
" bility have been called into existence. The only
" difference between the two cases is, that the laws
" of sunset have been thoroughly mastered ; whereas

" our knowledge as to the laws of fever, though
" very considerable, is as yet but partial and in-
" complete.* The 'abstract power of prediction,'
" —as Mr. Stuart Mill calls it,—is the one assump-
" tion, in every nook and corner of science. All
" scientific men take for granted—when they cease
" to do so they will cease to *be* scientific men—
" that a person of superhuman and adequate in-
" telligence, who should know accurately and fully
" all the various combinations and properties of
" matter which now exist, could predict infallibly
" the whole series of future phenomena. He could
" predict the future course of weather or of disease,
" with the same assurance with which men now
" predict the date of a coming eclipse. Pray God
" all day long—add fasting to your prayer if you
" like, and let all your fellow-Christians add *their*
" prayer and fasting to yours—in order that the
" said eclipse shall come a week earlier : do you
" suppose you will be heard ? Yet the pre-
" cise date of an eclipse is not more peremptorily
" fixed by the laws of nature, than is the precise
" issue of your daughter's fever. You do not ven-
" ture to doubt speculatively this fundamental
" doctrine of science : in our various scientific con-
" versations, my friend, you have always admitted it.
" But, like a true Englishman, you take refuge in
" an illogical compromise. You assume one doc-
" trine when you study science ; and another, its
" direct contradictory, when your child falls ill.
" And yet I am paying you too high a compliment :
" for you do not *profess* that this latter doctrine is
" *true*; you do not *profess* that your prayer to God

---

* "Ordinary Christians ask for fair weather and for rain, *but
they do not ask that water may run up hill;* while *the man of
science clearly sees* that the granting of one petition would be *just
as much an infringement of law* .... as the granting of the
other. Holding *the law* to be permanent, *he prays for neither.*"—
Professor Tyndall, quoted in "Church and World," p. 230.

" is *reasonable*, or can possibly be *efficacious* : your
" only defence is, that your reason is mastered and
" overborne by the combined effect of your religious
" and your parental emotion. As though you could
" please God—if indeed there be a Personal God
" at all—by acting in a manner which your reason
" condemns.

" 2. Well: you tell me you see your mistake;
" you will henceforth pray for *spiritual* blessings,
" and for them alone. Why you are still as unrea-
" sonable as you were before. Is not psychology
" then as truly a science as medicine ? You never
" doubted that it was, when you used to take such
" interest in the study of Reid and Hamilton. But
" if psychology *be* a science—if the conclusions
" whether of Hartley and Mill or of Hamilton and
" M'Cosh, have more value than the inventions of
" a fortune-teller or the dreams of a madman—
" *mental* phenomena proceed on fixed laws, no less
" inflexibly than *physical*. What then can possibly
" be your meaning, when you pray for what you
" call grace ? when you supplicate for help against
" what you call temptation? for growth in what
" you call virtue ? All these prayers imply in their
" very notion, that your God is constantly inter-
" fering with the course of mental phenomena. To
" talk as you do,—or at least to pray as you do,—
" is equivalent to saying in so many words—not that
" this or that school of psychologians is in error—
" but that there is no science of psychology at all;
" that there are no fixed laws of mind to be disco-
" vered by any one whomsoever; that the real agency
" at work, in causing our various thoughts, voli-
" tions, and emotions, is the unceasing and arbi-
" trary intervention of a Personal Creator and
" Sanctifier. Take your choice. Believe in science,
" or believe in the efficacy of prayer. But at least
" do not assume an intellectual position so obviously
" contemptible, as that of seeking to combine the two.

" 3. At least, you reply, you may exercise your
" *Free Will* for good or for evil, however powerless
" your God may be to assist you in the combat. On
" the contrary, I rejoin, this figment of Free Will is
" even more directly unscientific, than the super-
" stition of prayer. The very foundation of all
" science, as every one well knows, is this great
" truth, that the same phenomenal antecedents are
" invariably succeeded by the same phenomenal
" consequents. Now the notion of Free Will directly
" and (as it were) unblushingly contradicts this
" fundamental truth. When you say that your will
" is free, your very meaning is that—the very same
" phenomenal antecedents being supposed, both phy-
" sical and mental—you possess a real power of
" choosing *what* mental *consequent* shall ensue. How
" amazing,—not that a priest-ridden Ultramontane
" or an ignorant rustic—but that you, an educated
" and scientific gentleman, can have been blind to
" so extravagant an inconsistency !
  " 4. After this it is hardly worth while to make
" one more remark, which I will not however omit.
" The Christian religion, in particular, is grounded
" on an allegation of *Miracles*. But Miracles, it is
" plain, constitute the same anti-scientific absurdity
" in the material world, which Free Will constitutes
" in the mental. To believe the existence of Miracles,
" is ipso facto to disbelieve phenomenal uniformity ;
" and to disbelieve phenomenal uniformity, is to
" reject the very possibility of science."
  We have stated all this in its full extent ; because
we are very desirous that our readers should understand, *what* the argument means if it means anything at all. It would be most unjust to doubt that
many scientific men, who carry it to a certain extent,
would be appalled at the very thought of embracing
that full conclusion in which it issues : and they
may be greatly benefited therefore, by being brought
to understand what that full conclusion is. More-

over (as we have already said) it is of great moment that Christians in general, and Catholics in particular, should understand how tremendous is the danger lurking under a few plausible generalities; that they should see once for all how vain is all thought of concession and compromise; and that they should gird themselves for an internecine conflict. Lastly, we should be extremely glad if, by exhibiting the urgency of the crisis, we could induce competent Christian writers to enter more fully on the work of reply than they have hitherto done. There is no part, or hardly any part, of the true answer to these irreligious arguments, which has not been already stated incidentally here or there by some Christian thinker; but we greatly desiderate a far more systematic, comprehensive, and emphatic consideration of the whole matter, than has hitherto been afforded. Even were there far less than there is of vigour and conclusive argument in Dr. Gilbert's discourses, he would deserve our sincerest gratitude for drawing methodical attention to the subject. But he has done much more than this. He has failed indeed, we think, to grasp the full extent of that irreligious theory, which Catholics have to encounter; but he has given many satisfactory, and some quite admirable, answers to the particular objections which he has considered.

We have seldom seen so disappointing a work as the Duke of Argyll's, which we have also named at the head of this article. In saying this however, we are very far indeed from intending simply to disparage it; on the contrary, it is the rare excellence of some individual passages, which leads us to expect elsewhere what we do not find. Some of the defects which we lament are no doubt attributable to the volume's fragmentary character; and we certainly much regret that, instead of republishing a number of separate papers, the Duke did not take the trouble of working up his materials into one harmonious whole. Still the intellectual faults exhibited, we cannot but think, lie deeper than the mere form of his production. There are many signs indeed in the volume of his possessing, not only great fairness and justice of view, but also a real capacity for profound thought; yet the signs are not less conspicuous of his not having duly evoked into exercise this latter capacity. He impresses us as having given too large a proportion of his time to acquiring knowledge, and too small a proportion to digesting and reflecting on the materials thus obtained. The extent of his knowledge is certainly very remarkable; and many of his incidental observations display real originality and genius.

We cannot give a better specimen, both of the Duke's excellences and of his defects, than his treatment of the first irreligious objection above recounted. We will begin however by soliciting our readers' most careful attention to his truly admirable remarks, on the utter emptiness and baselessness of one cowardly intellectual subterfuge, to which resort has at times been attempted. And in this, as in our other quotations, we italicise certain passages, to which we solicit our readers' particular attention. Some writers then have proclaimed the existence of a certain (as it were) impassable gulf, between the respective realms of theology and secular science. It is by means of this subterfuge, that minimising Catholics would shirk the Church's authority throughout the whole sphere of secular speculation;* and it is by the same means, that many scientific men excuse themselves from the charge of injuring religion, when they admit irreligious principles into the sphere of their own science.

---

* [The Church, I need hardly explain, does not claim authority within the sphere of secular science, except so far as scientific theories bear, directly or indirectly, on the Deposit of Faith.]

And so we see [says the Duke] the men of Theology coming out to parley with the men of science,—a white flag in their hands, and saying, "*If you will let us alone, we will do the same by you.* Keep to your own province; do not enter ours. The reign of Law which you proclaim, we admit—outside these walls, but not within them :—let there be peace between us." But this will never do. *There can be no such treaty dividing the domain of Truth. Every one Truth is connected with every other Truth in this great Universe of God.*

It is against a certain real danger, that some one would erect a feeble barrier by defending the position, that Science and Religion may be, and ought to be, kept entirely separate ;—that they belong to wholly different spheres of thought, and *that the ideas which prevail in the one province have no relation to those which prevail in the other.* This is a doctrine offering many temptations to many minds. It is grateful to scientific men who are afraid of being thought hostile to Religion. It is grateful to religious men who are afraid of being thought to be afraid of Science. To these, and to all who are troubled to reconcile what they have been taught to believe with what they have come to know, this doctrine affords a natural and convenient escape. *There is but one objection to it—but that is the fatal objection—that it is not true.*

The spiritual world and the intellectual world are not separated after this fashion : and the notion that they are so separated does but encourage men to accept in each, ideas which will at last be found to be false in both. The truth is, that there is no branch of human inquiry, however purely physical, which is more than the word "branch" implies ;—none which is not connected through endless ramifications with every other,—*and especially with that which is the root and centre of them all.* If He who formed the mind be one with Him who is the Orderer of all things concerning which that mind is occupied, *there can be no end to the points of contact* between our different conceptions of them, of Him, and of ourselves.

The instinct which impels us to seek for harmony in the truths of Science and the truths of Religion, is a higher instinct and a truer one than the disposition which leads us to evade the difficulty by pretending that there is no relation between them. For, after all, *it is a pretence and nothing more. No man who thoroughly accepts a principle in the philosophy of Nature which he feels to be inconsistent with a doctrine of Religion, can help having his belief in that doctrine shaken and undermined.* We may believe, and we must believe, both in Nature and in Religion, many things which we cannot understand ; but *we cannot really believe two propositions which are felt to be contradictory.* It helps us nothing in such a difficulty, to say that the one proposition belongs to Reason and the other proposition belongs to Faith.

The endeavour to reconcile them is a necessity of the mind. We are right in thinking that *if they are both indeed true they can be reconciled, and if they really are fundamentally opposed they cannot both be true* (pp. 53–55).

It will have been observed with much interest, how frankly the Duke, in the course of this extract, admits theology to be " the root and centre of all" sciences. Such an opinion indeed cannot be avoided by any clear-headed man, who believes that there *is* such a science as theology, and who will look facts in the face. But then there are so many clear-headed men who do *not* believe that there is such a science as theology; and so many others, who will *not* look facts in the face.

After this preliminary and most important introduction, the Duke states with extreme force and candour the anti-religious objection to which we referred above; and here again his language is so masterly and so clear, that we cannot refrain from quoting it in extenso. He refers then to

The conclusion to which the language of some scientific men is evidently pointing, that *great general Laws inexorable in their application*, and Causes in endless chain of invariable sequence, are the governing powers in Nature, and that they *leave no room for any special direction or providential ordering of events. If this be true, it is vain to deny its bearing on Religion. What then can be the use of prayer ? Can Laws hear us ? Can they change, or can they suspend themselves ?* These questions cannot but arise, and they require an answer. It is said of a late eminent Professor and clergyman of the English Church,* who was deeply imbued with these opinions on the place occupied by Law in the economy of Nature, that he went on nevertheless, preaching high doctrinal sermons from the pulpit until his death. He did so on the ground that propositions which were contrary to his reason were not necessarily beyond his faith. The inconsistencies of the human mind are indeed unfathomable ; and there are men so constituted *as honestly to suppose that they can divide themselves into two spiritual beings, one of whom is sceptical, and the other is believing.* But such men are rare—happily for Religion, and not less happily

---

* We imagine that reference is here made to the late Rev. Baden Powell.—ED. D. R.

for science. *No healthy intellect, no earnest spirit, can rest in such self-betrayal.* Accordingly we find many men now facing the consequences to which they have given their intellectual assent, and *taking their stand upon the ground that prayer to God has no other value or effect than so far as it may be a good way of preaching to ourselves.* It is a useful and helpful exercise for our own spirits, but it is nothing more. But how can they pray who have come to this? *Can it ever be useful or helpful to believe a lie?* That which has been threatened as the worst of all spiritual evils, would then become the constant attitude of our "religion," the habitual condition of our worship. *This must be as bad science, as it is bad religion* (pp. 58—60).

The Duke then proceeds, as our imaginary objector proceeded above, to show the impossibility of such a distinction as some have attempted to draw between physical and mental phenomena :—

The compromise now offered by some philosophers is this—that although the course of *external nature* is unalterable, yet possibly the phenomena of *mind and character* may be changed by the Divine Agency. But will this reasoning bear analysis? Can the distinction it assumes be maintained? Whatever difficulties there may be in reconciling the ideas of Law and of Volition, are difficulties which apply equally to the Worlds of Matter and of Mind. *The Mind is as much subject to Law as the Body is.* The reign of Law is over all; and if its dominion be really incompatible with the agency of Volition, Human or Divine, then the Mind is as inaccessible to that agency as material things (p. 61).

This admirable statement of the difficulty raised our hopes to the highest pitch ; and we fully expected to find the objection answered, in the same satisfactory and masterly way in which it had been stated. In this hope we were disappointed. The previous extracts have shown, both how clearly the Duke is able to see the opposing argument, and also how heartily he dislikes the conclusion to which it tends ; but we close the volume in absolute uncertainty how he would himself reply to it.

Various other portions of the work will come before us, for the expression both of assent and dissent, as our discussion proceeds; but since the last chapter, on "the reign of Law in Politics," is

wholly external to our present scope, we must not
omit here to give it its due meed of praise. It is
both original and powerful; and we are able more
unreservedly to agree with it, than with any other
of the seven Essays.

Mr. M'Coll's Essay is written generally in the
best possible spirit, and is not without incidental
remarks of much force and vigour; yet on the
whole he has neither done justice, we think, to the
strength of his opponents' view, nor yet to the
strength of his own. We regret also to find,
towards the beginning, language savouring of that
illogical attempt—which the Duke of Argyll so
excellently rebukes—to deny all contact between the
respective spheres of theology and secular science.

Science [says our author], not content with *toleration and good
neighbourhood* on the part of the Church, aspires to dictate the
articles of her creed, and prescribe her very forms of devotion.
Of this aggressive disposition on the part of science, the recent
attack on special prayer is an instance. The prayer against the
cholera and the cattle-plague *cannot be accused of encroaching on
any of the rights and privileges of science.* It moves in another
sphere; and is simply based on our recognition of a God, whose
Love is infinite, and whose Power is equal to His Love. It is
strictly framed on Bacon's advice, "being kept within its own
province," and not venturing on any "excursions into the limits
of physical causes." Yet Natural Science, in so far as it is repre-
sented by Professor Tyndall, turns round upon us with a scowl,
and tells us that, in the opinion of the great majority of sane
persons, "we are little better than fools for believing that our
prayers can avail to stop the progress of the pestilence" (p. 414).

Surely the Church does make an aggression—a
most laudable and just one doubtless, but still an
aggression — on the domain of physical science,
when she proclaims that prayer to God often alters
the course of phenomena. Surely "the course of
phenomena" is precisely the one object-matter of
experimental science. How can it be said then that
the Church exhibits "toleration and good neighbourhood" to that science, when she dogmatizes on
its one object-matter? The "abstract power of

predicting phenomena " (see p. 5 of this article)
is claimed as the very foundation of experimental
science, by a large number of her most ardent
votaries ; and the Church, in teaching the efficacy
of prayer, directly assails that foundation. Yet
Mr. M'Coll says that theology " cannot " even " be
accused of encroaching on any of the rights and
privileges of science." Surely such an " accusation " is not only possible, but is thoroughly well
founded ; except indeed so far as the word " en-
croachment " implies an *undue* claim of control.
She claims to control physical science, and her
claim is a most proper one. Consider the two following propositions :—Prop. 1 : " There is an abstract
power of scientifically predicting all future phenomena " : here is a *scientific* proposition, true or
false. Prop. 2 : " The future course of phenomena
will be affected indefinitely by God's Intervention ;
whether He acts simply on His own inscrutable
Will, or whether in answer to the prayer of Most
Holy Mary, of Angels, of Saints, of men on earth " :
here is a *theological* proposition, true or false. Mr.
M'Coll speaks as though these two propositions
respectively belonged to two spheres, which have
no points of mutual contact. How strange ! Why
one is the logical contradictory of the other. He
who holds the former must reject the latter, and he
who holds the latter must reject the former. To
say that theology and science are mutually *independent,* seems to us the one position more obviously illogical and untenable than any other that
can be devised. Sacred science must be granted
superiority over secular ; or else secular science
will assume superiority over sacred. And if any
Christian shrinks from claiming for theology such
superiority,—however pious and admirable may be
his intentions, he is in fact betraying the cause
which he wishes to serve.*

---

* We have several times drawn attention to Pius IX.'s strong

At the present day many, even among Catholics, are in the habit of conceding very readily that, in times past, "theologians intruded into the province of science"; and we cannot be surprised therefore, that Mr. M'Coll, who is not a Catholic, has taken the accusation for granted (p. 412). It would certainly be over-bold to assert confidently a negative; but at least, before we admit the truth of so grave an accusation, we desire to see some attempt at substantiating it. The only proof to which Mr. M'Coll refers, is the case of Galileo; and on that case we are perfectly confident, that the theologians were right in principle from first to last.*

So much then on the three works which we have named at the head of our article. For ourselves, as we have already said, we can aspire to nothing more than an exhibition of the merest skeleton of outline; which, should it meet with approval, might be filled up and expanded, by those who are more fitted for the task both from natural qualifications and from scientific accomplishments.

We will beg our readers to look back at the four objections which we are to meet. They are directed respectively (1) against the efficacy of prayer for temporal blessings; (2) against the possibility of Divine Grace; (3) against Free Will; and (4) against Miracles. They are of very unequal force; and we consider the *last* indeed to be frivolous in the extreme. We will take them however in the order in which they have been stated. We admit of course at starting, what the Church has ever taught; viz., that God has impressed on each portion of matter certain intrinsic properties, and a certain definite unchanged agency of its own. Truth obliges us

---

language in his Munich Brief, on the Church's authority over physical science.

* [Galileo's case has been since treated by me at length, in the "Dublin Review" for April and July, 1871.]

indeed further to maintain, that He has retained in His own hands the power of suspending or even reversing the action of such properties ; yet, as regards the first two objections on our list, there is no necessity whatever for insisting on this qualification. On the contrary, we are fully prepared to concede for argument's sake, that He never does interfere with the properties of matter ; that He never does reverse their natural agency ; that the laws of nature are absolutely fixed, and the sequence of phenomena absolutely uniform. We contend that— even were this hypothesis ever so unreservedly true, —there would still be no cogency whatever in those irreligious arguments, which are adduced to sustain the two first objections above recited. Of these, we will treat the former in detail ; and afterwards apply very easily to the second, what will have been already said in reply to the first. The third and fourth shall afterwards be considered fully and carefully, on their respective grounds.

Let it be conceded then for argument's sake, that the whole material world proceeds unexceptionally on the basis of phenomenal uniformity ; that the laws of nature are most absolutely fixed. Firstly we say, it does not follow or tend ever so distantly to follow, because they are *fixed*, that they proceed independently of God's constant and unremitting " premovement."* Nay secondly we say that—putting aside all the proofs of revealed religion—physical phenomena alone, if duly considered, give even greater probability to the religious than to the irreligious

---

* What we mean by this word will immediately appear. We do not say " premotion," because this word has a special sense in the Thomistic philosophy, totally distinct from that here intended. There is a certain " concursus " also, which Catholics consider to be constantly put forth by God, in default of which the whole creation would sink back into nothingness : but the " premovement " of which we speak in the text is a great deal more than this.

conclusion. But if such Divine premovement be admitted, then the efficacy of man's prayer for temporal blessings is the dictate of reason no less truly than of faith. Since however it is essential that the reader shall carry with him a clear notion of what we mean by this Divine premovement, we trust he will pardon us much grotesqueness and some lengthiness of illustration. However grotesque may be the supposition we are going to make, we believe it will be found singularly adapted to the only purpose for which we use it: the purpose of enabling our readers to understand distinctly what we mean.

We begin then with imagining two mice, endowed however with quasi-human or semi-human intelligence, enclosed within a grand pianoforte, but prevented in some way or other from interfering with the free play of its machinery. From time to time they are delighted with the strains of choice music. One of the two considers these to result from some agency external to the instrument; but the other, having a more philosophical mind, rises to the conception of fixed laws and of phenomenal uniformity. " Science as yet," he says, " is but in its infancy; but I have already made one or two important discoveries. Every sound which reaches us is preceded by a certain vibration of these strings. The same string invariably produces the same sound ; and that louder or more gentle, accordingly as the vibration may be more or less intense. Sounds of a more composite character result, when two or more of the strings vibrate together; and here again the sound produced, as far as I am able to discover, is precisely a compound of those sounds, which would have resulted from the various component strings vibrating separately. Then there is a further sequence which I have observed : for each vibration is preceded by a stroke from a corresponding hammer; and the string vibrates more intensely, in proportion as the hammer's stroke is more forcible. Thus far I have already prosecuted my researches. And so much at least is evident even now; viz., that the sounds proceed, not from any external and arbitrary agency —from the intervention e.g. of any higher will— but from the uniform operation of fixed laws. These laws may be explored by intelligent mice; and to their exploration I shall devote my life." Even from this inadequate illustration, you see the general conclusion which we wish to enforce. A sound has been produced through a certain intermediate chain of fixed laws: but this fact does not tend ever so distantly to establish the conclusion, that there is no human premovement acting continuously at one end of that chain.

Imagination however has no limits. We may very easily suppose therefore, that some instrument is discovered, producing music immeasurably more heavenly and transporting than that of the pianoforte; but for that very reason immeasurably more vast in size and more complex in machinery. We will call this imaginary instrument a " polychordon," as we are not aware that there is any existing claimant of that name. In this polychordon, the intermediate links—between the player's premove·ment on one hand and the resulting sound on the other,—are no longer two, but two hundred. We further suppose—imagination (as before said) being boundless—that some human being or other is unintermittently playing on this polychordon; but playing on it just what airs may strike his fancy at the moment. Well: successive generations of philosophical mice have actually traced one hundred and fifty of the two hundred phenomenal sequences, through whose fixed and invariable laws the sound is produced. The colony of mice, shut up within, are in the highest spirits at the success which has crowned the scientific labour of their leading thinkers; and the most eminent of these addresses an assembly. " We have long known that the laws of our musical universe are immutably fixed ; but we have now discovered a far larger number of those laws, than our ancestors could have imagined *capable* of discovery. Let us redouble our efforts. I fully expect that our grandchildren will be able to predict as accurately, for an indefinitely preceding period, the succession of melodies with which we are to be delighted, as we now predict the hours of sunrise and sunset.* One thing, at all events, is now absolutely incontrovertible. As to the notion of there being some agency *external* to the polychordon,— intervening with arbitrary and capricious will to produce the sounds we experience,—this is a long-exploded superstition ; a mere dream and dotage of the past. The progress of science has put it on one side, and never again can it return to disturb our philosophical progress."

The whole illustration will have made, we think, abundantly clear, both the meaning, and the truth, of that proposition for which we are contending. Two hundred absolutely fixed laws intervene, between the player's premovement and the resulting sound : but this fact does not tend ever so remotely to show, that there is not an intelligent player ; or that his premovement is not absolutely unremitting. And in like manner,—though phenomenal laws the most strictly and rigorously uniform existed throughout the realm of nature,—such a fact would not tend ever so remotely to show what irreligious men pretend : it would not tend ever so remotely to show, that those laws are not at each moment directed, to this purpose or to that, by an *immediate and uncontrolled Divine Premovement*. God's real ends cannot be more inscrutable to us, according to the Christian's belief, than would be the ends of a human performer to the mice within this supposed poly-

---

* The polychordon, if the reader pleases, may be supposed to have a glass cover, through which light penetrates.

chordon. Indeed we do know so much as this, that His ends are those of Infinite Wisdom and Holiness. And as a player on the polychordon may readily be induced, at the smallest request of a little child, to produce this particular musical result rather than some other; so the heartfelt prayer of the humblest Christian may powerfully affect God's premovement of the physical world. We are not here arguing, be it observed, that the truth *is* so; we are but saying, that the mere fact of phenomenal uniformity does not ever so remotely tend to show that the truth is *not* so.

We now then proceed to our second proposition. Even apart from the motives of credibility exhibited by revealed religion—physical phenomena taken by themselves would make it (we maintain) more probable than not, that God does unintermittently premove, in accordance with His inscrutable purposes, those fixed laws which pervade the external world. Before drawing out an argument which appears to us far more cogent than any other in behalf of this conclusion—we will enter on a preliminary matter of no inconsiderable importance. We will here then draw the attention of our readers to a thesis, which occupies almost as much of the Duke of Argyll's volume as all his others put together; and which he certainly handles with signal power and success. It has not unfrequently been held, that the investigation of *physical* causes interferes with the due appreciation of *final;* that the habit of exploring phenomenal *sequences* is greatly injurious to the habit of recognising phenomenal *design.* Now if by this be merely meant that many scientific men, through a certain deplorable narrowness and prejudice, close their eyes to a large number of undoubted facts, there is much truth, no doubt, in the allegation. But those who use such language, generally mean much more than this. They seem to mean, that the progress of physical science has really weakened the *argument* derivable from nature, for the existence of design in the material world. No supposition can be more scientifically unfounded than this; and we wish we had space to quote all the masterly passages in which the Duke refutes it. We must confine ourselves however to two extracts; though the first will be of considerable length. The italics, of course, are our own :—

And yet scientific men sometimes tell us that "we must be very cautious how we ascribe intention to Nature. Things do fit into each other, no doubt, as if they were designed; but all we know about them is that these correspondences exist, and that they seem to be the result of physical laws of development and growth." Very likely; but how these correspondences have arisen, and are daily arising, is not the question, and it is immaterial how that question may be answered. Do those correspondences exist, or do they not? *The perception of them by our mind is as much a fact, as the sight or touch of the things in which they appear.* They may have been produced by growth,—they may have been the result of a process of development,—but it is not the less the development of a mental purpose. *It is the end subserved that we absolutely know. What alone is doubtful and obscure is precisely that which alone we are told is the legitimate object of our research,*—viz., the means by which that end has been attained. Take one instance out of millions. The poison of a deadly snake—let us for a moment consider what this is. It is a secretion of definite chemical properties which have reference, not only—not even mainly—to the organism of the animal in which it is developed, but specially to the organism of another animal which it is intended to destroy. Some naturalists have a vague sort of notion that, as regards merely mechanical weapons or organs of attack, they may be developed by use,—that legs may become longer by fast running, teeth sharper and longer by much biting. Be it so : this law of growth, if it exist, is but itself an instrument whereby purpose is fulfilled. But *how will this law of growth adjust a poison in one animal with such subtle knowledge of the organisation of another*, that the deadly virus shall in a few minutes curdle the blood, benumb the nerves, and rush in upon the citadel of life? *There is but one explanation—a Mind, having minute and perfect knowledge of the structure of both, has designed the one to be capable of inflicting death upon the other.* This mental purpose and resolve is *the one thing* which our intelligence perceives with direct and intuitive recognition. The method of creation, by means of which this purpose has been carried into effect, is utterly unknown.

Perhaps no illustration more striking of this principle was ever presented, than in the curious volume published by Mr. Darwin on the " Fertilisation of Orchids." It appears that the fertilisation of almost all Orchids is dependent on the transport of the pollen from one flower to another by means of insects. It appears, further, that the structure of these flowers is elaborately contrived, so as to secure the certainty and effectiveness of this operation. Mr. Darwin's work is devoted to tracing in detail what these contrivances are. To a large extent they are purely mechanical, and can be traced with as much clearness and certainty as the different parts of which a steam-engine is composed. *The complication and ingenuity of these contrivances almost exceed belief.* " Moth-traps and spring-guns set on these grounds," might be the motto of the Orchids. There are baits to tempt the nectar-loving Lepidoptera, with rich odours exhaled at night, and lustrous colours to shine by day ; there are channels of approach along which they are surely guided, so as to compel them to pass by certain spots; there are adhesive plasters nicely adjusted to fit their probosces, or to catch their brows ; there are hair-triggers carefully set in their necessary path, communicating with explosive shells, which project the pollen-stalks with unerring aim upon their bodies. There are, in short, an infinitude of adjustments, for an idea of which I must refer my readers to Mr. Darwin's inimitable powers of observation and description—adjustments all contrived so as to secure the accurate conveyance of the pollen of the one flower to its precise destination in the structure of another.

Now there are two questions which present themselves, when we examine such a mechanism as this. *The first is, What is the use of the various parts, or their relation to each other with reference to the purpose of the whole ?* The second question is, How were those parts made, and out of what materials? *It is the first of these questions—that is to say, the use, object, intention, or purpose of the different parts of the plant,—which Darwin sets himself instinctively to answer first ; and it is this which he does answer with precision and success.* The second question,—that is to say, how those parts came to be developed, and out of what " primordial elements " they have been derived in their present shapes, and converted to their present uses—this is a question which Darwin does also attempt to solve, but the solution of which is *in the highest degree difficult and uncertain.* It is curious to observe the language which this most advanced disciple of pure naturalism instinctively uses, when he has to describe the complicated structure of this curious order of plants. " Caution in ascribing intentions to nature " does not seem to occur to him as possible. *Intention is the one thing which he does see, and which, when he does not see, he seeks for diligently until he finds it.* He exhausts every form of words and of illustration by which intention or mental purpose can be described. " Contrivance "—" curious contrivance "—" beautiful contrivance,"—these are expressions which recur over and over again. Here is one sentence describing the parts of a particular species: "The Labellum is developed into a long nectary, *in order* to attract Lepidoptera ; and we shall presently give reasons for suspecting that the nectar is *purposely* so lodged that it can be sucked only slowly, *in order* to give time for the curious chemical quality of the viscid matter setting hard and dry." Nor are these words used in any sense different from that in which they are applicable to the works of man's contrivance—to the instruments we use or invent for carrying into effect our own preconceived designs. On the contrary, human instruments are often selected as the aptest illustrations both of the object in view, and of the means taken to effect it. Of one particular structure Mr. Darwin says :—" This contrivance of the guiding ridges may be compared to the little instrument sometimes used for guiding a thread into the eye of a needle." Again, referring to the precautions taken to compel the insects to come to the proper spot, in order to have the " pollinia " attached to their bodies, Mr. Darwin says :—" Thus we have the rostellum partially closing the mouth of the nectary, *like a trap placed in a run for game,*—and the trap so complex and perfect !" But this is not all. The idea of special use, as the controlling principle of construction, is so impressed on Mr. Darwin's mind, that, in every detail of structure, however singular or obscure, he has absolute faith that in this lies the ultimate explanation. If an organ is largely developed, it is because some special purpose is to be fulfilled. If it is aborted or rudimentary, it is because that purpose is no longer to be subserved. In the case of another species whose structure is very singular, Mr. Darwin had great difficulty in discovering how the mechanism was meant to work, so as to effect the purpose. At last he made it out, and of the clue which led to the discovery he says :—" The strange position of the Labellum perched on the summit of the column, *ought to have shown me that here was the place for experiment.* I ought to have scorned the notion that the Labellum was thus placed *for no good purpose.* I neglected this plain guide, and for a long time completely failed to understand the flower " (pp. 35—42).

The laws of nature are employed in the system of nature in a manner precisely analogous to that in which we ourselves employ them. The difficulties and obstructions which are presented by one law in the way of accomplishing a given purpose, are met and overcome exactly on the same principle on which they are met and overcome by Man—viz., by knowledge of other laws, and by resource in applying them—that is, *by ingenuity in mechanical contrivance.* It cannot be too much insisted on, that *this is a conclusion of pure Science.* The relation which an organic structure bears to its purpose *in Nature,* can be recognised as certainly as the same relation between a machine and its purpose *in human art.* It is absurd to maintain, for example, that the purpose of the cellular arrangement of material in combining lightness with strength, is a purpose *legitimately cognisable by Science in the Menai Bridge*, but is not *as legitimately cognisable when it is seen in Nature*, actually serving the same use. The little barnacles which crust the rocks at low tide, and which to live there at all must be able to resist the surf, have the building of their shells constructed strictly with reference to this necessity. It is a structure all hollowed and chambered *on the plan which engineers have so lately discovered* as an arrangement of material by which the power of resisting strain or pressure is multiplied in an extraordinary degree. That shell *is as pure a bit of mechanics as the bridge*, both being structures in which the same arrangement is adapted to the same end (pp. 101–2).

There is another evidence of design furnished by nature, on which writers like Paley have laid no stress at all; but which is in truth as argumentatively available as the former. "Mere *ornament or beauty*," says the Duke (p. 196), "is in itself an object, a purpose, and an end."

Some of the most beautiful forms in Nature [he proceeds] are the shells of the marine Mollusca, and many of them are the richest, too, in surface-ornament. But, prodigal of beauty as the Ocean now is in the creatures which it holds, its wealth was even greater and more abounding in times when there was no man to gather them. The shells and corals of the old Silurian Sea were as elaborate and as richly carved as those which we now admire : and the noble Ammonites of the Secondary ages must have been glorious things indeed. Even now there is abundant evidence that although Man was intended to admire beauty, beauty was not intended only for man's admiration. Nowhere is ornament more richly given, nowhere is it seen *more separate from the use*, than in those organisms of whose countless millions the microscope alone enables a few men for a few moments to see a few examples (pp. 198–9).

Our readers, we are sure, will thank us for putting before them a still more beautiful passage to the same effect, from a long-forgotten article in the old "British Critic." At the same time we disclaim sympathy with its author's various hits against Paley's particular line of argument :—

There is no purpose of mere animal life that might not have

been answered quite as well without such a thing as beauty or grandeur being in the number of created things. A very few, and, weighed in some scales, very trifling changes, would have made the difference—a difference to them that are blessed with eyes that see, and ears that hear, but no difference to the consistent utilitarian. *A very little change in the constitution and law of light would have made all nature of a dusky brown, or a sickly yellow:* a very slightly different atmosphere would have excluded the sight and knowledge of the sun, moon, and stars, without an utter exclusion of their light. Trees, shrubs, and herbs of the field, might have been all one shape and hue : the earth a dead level, with just fall enough for rivers and canals. The natural geography of the globe might have run in lines of latitude and longitude like the boundaries in the United States. Let some one write a book on *the Catholicism of nature*—its rites and ceremonies—its symbols—*its infinite redundance of ornament—its boundless variety of form*—its ceaseless importunity of praise. Let him exclude from count all that may be brought under the head of "utility," and there will be a still *countless remainder of superfluous beauties.* His work will have a sort of parallelism with Paley's more Protestant undertaking ; but he need not fear encroaching on the province of that ingenious writer. On the contrary, he must purposely reject whatever can come under the Paleyan formula. His business will be with those features and qualities of the creation which are useless on mere physical principles ; and only useful, and probably intentional, for their effect on the human soul, *as outwardly conspiring with inward instincts to produce and cherish the sense of the beautiful, the awful, and the sublime* (Oct. 1841, pp. 468-9).

Now it would carry us entirely away from our course of argument, if we attempted here to consider how far natural phenomena, taken by themselves, would prove (or even render probable) the proposition, that their Designer possesses the attribute of *Infinity ;* or again of *Sanctity.* But we are here urging, that at all events they make His *Existence* absolutely certain ; the Existence of a real designing Mind. This is the one most certain of all lessons which physical science teaches ; and this bears importantly on our present subject. The Creator originally fixed the laws of nature, with a view to certain momentous purposes : it is surely then far more probable than not, that He *still* actively occupies Himself in the advancement of these purposes. It is far more probable, we say, that He still actively forwards those ends which He has at heart, than that He rests content with such promotion of them, as was involved in the very fact of creation. A Creator, self-banished from active interference with the operation of those laws which He has Himself ordained, is a possible indeed, but surely an almost incredible, hypothesis.

We now proceed to the argument on which we are principally to dwell, as supporting belief in God's constant and unremitting premovement of natural laws. And we commence this argument by inquiring, what is that imaginable conclusion of physical science, which *would* disprove the doctrine we advocate. We answer most readily : *the abstract power of indefinite prediction.* Our imaginary objector took for granted, that any person of superhuman and adequate intelligence, who should know thoroughly and accurately all the various properties and combinations of matter which now exist, could predict infallibly the whole series of future phenomena. If this hypothesis were established as true, there would at once result a final and absolute *disproof* of that great verity which we are defending; a final and absolute disproof of every notion, that God does unintermittently premove the laws of nature. Let us suppose for a moment, that we have no means of information on the subject, except physical science itself. Were this the case,—so far as scientific investigations have added greater or less probability to the supposition that there exists an abstract power of indefinite prediction—precisely so far they would have added greater or less probability to the supposition, that phenomena proceed independently of God's premovement. Here then we are at the very heart of that unspeakably momentous question which we are discussing.

Before going further then, let us make it more clear and unmistakable that we have correctly stated the point at issue. And firstly, when we speak of "indefinite prediction," what do we mean by this word "indefinite"? We use it as contra-distinguished from the word "brief." Let us go back for a moment to our imaginary polychordon. It may well be supposed—considering the extraordinary complication which we ascribe to its machinery— that some ten minutes e.g. shall elapse, between the human premovement and its musical result. Philo-sophical mice then—those who have investigated one hundred and fifty out of the two hundred inter-vening links—might be well able to predict quite infallibly, at least seven minutes beforehand, the coming melody. And so as to physical facts. We believe Sir H. Fitzroy was at last obliged to give up his attempted prognostication of weather, from the mischievous or amusing blunders into which he con-stantly fell. Yet we can well suppose, as science advances, that a coming storm might be predicted with almost infallible accuracy, say twenty-four hours before the event. And yet it would none the less be true that, as man (according to our supposi-tion) plays constantly on the polychordon, so God is constantly playing (so to speak) on the vast in-strument of nature.

But now take a different type of musical instru-ments. The power of imagination, as we have more than once said, is boundless. Let us suppose then some huge instrument, constructed on the principle of a barrel-organ : set for ten years to a continuance of successive and ever-recurring airs, and with mechanical provision for its constant movement throughout that period. Our philosophical mice, if shut up within such an instrument as this, might undoubtedly arrive at an indefinite power of pre-dicting their future musical entertainment. If in five years' time they had successfully explored and studied the machinery, the last five years would furnish an uninterrupted fulfilment of their scientific predictions. And from such a circumstance they might most legitimately and irresistibly infer,—not merely that their instrument (like the polychordon) acts on fixed laws ;—but also that (*un*like the polychordon) it is independent of any arbitrary movement from without. There is no external player, they most logically infer, who unintermittently premoves the machinery for his own purposes. Undoubtedly therefore, if any class of phenomena be abstractedly capable of indefinite scientific prediction, this class of phenomena is *not* premoved by Almighty God.

Here then is the vital and essential issue of our present investigation. How far, we inquire, has the course of science (taken by itself) added probability to the supposition, that there is an abstract scientific possibility of indefinitely predicting the future course of all external phenomena ? Most assuredly science has not approximated to *proving* such abstract possibility : but we really believe more than this. We believe that the march of scientific progress has been in such a direction, that (on scientific grounds alone) the abstract possibility of such indefinite prediction is a more improbable hypothesis now, than it was two centuries ago. For consider. What can be more amazing than the present rapid advance of scientific truth ? " The enlargement of the circle of secular knowledge just now is simply a bewilderment ; and the more so, because it has the promise of continuing, and with greater rapidity and more signal results."* The speculative and the practical results of science succeed each other with a rapidity, which almost takes away one's breath. Take some inquirer of the Seventeenth Century, earnestly devoted to scientific pursuits, and possessing no firm grasp of religious truth. Suppose such a man had been

---

* Cardinal Newman's " Apologia."

authoritatively told of the astounding development which science was to receive in this Nineteenth Century. If there is one augury rather than another which such an inquirer would most confidently have made, it would be that the sphere of *scientific prediction* must by this time have received an incredible enlargement. And yet what are the facts? The more astounding you consider the rapidity with which science advances, so much the more astounding must you consider one further fact. We mean the fact, that this rapid advance *has not brought with it, in any one fresh department, any power whatever of indefinite prediction.* Astronomical facts were from the very first, to a large extent, capable of indefinite prediction; and science has no doubt in some degree enlarged the sphere of that capability. Science has enabled men e.g. to predict eclipses; the periodical return of comets; and certain other astronomical phenomena. But take such particulars as are relevant to the present inquiry, how widely different is the case! At what period of her existence was the Church in the habit of praying against comets and eclipses? On the contrary, what *are* those temporal evils from which Christians have besought deliverance? Famine, disease, unseasonable weather, war, shipwreck, extreme poverty, and the like. There is not one of these, in regard to which there are the faintest signs that it will hereafter be capable of indefinite scientific prediction. The Church's supplications may still be put forth by the most scientific Catholic, with as simple faith and fervour as by the most ignorant of rustics. "Ut morbos auferat, famem depellat, aperiat carceres, vincula dissolvat, peregrinantibus reditum, infirmantibus sanitatem, navigantibus portum salutis indulgeat,"—these are blessings which a scientific Catholic of the Nineteenth Century, no less than of the First, recognises without the slightest perplexity as obtainable from God through prayer. It is surely most remarkable, that the whole of this has been as it were charmed ground, proof against all the incursions of advancing science.

Indeed the contrast between astronomy and other sciences admits perhaps of being dwelt on more particularly. From the earliest periods, mankind must have been struck with the broad difference of action between what we may call respectively *cosmical* and *earthly* phenomena : the former proceeding on a course so steady, equable, and amenable to calculation ; the latter so apparently variable and capricious. By cosmical phenomena, we mean such as the hours of sunrise and sunset ; of moonrise and moonset ; the respective apparent position of the heavenly bodies, &c. &c. By earthly phenomena we mean such as the weather ; the violence and direction of the wind ; the progress of disease ; and others of a similar kind. The discovery of Copernicanism placed these two phenomenal classes in far more striking contrast. It appears that cosmical phenomena are produced by an incredibly vast machinery, in which this earth plays a very subordinate part ; whereas earthly phenomena are due in great measure to agencies, which act exclusively within the region of our planet. From the very first therefore, there was a real presumption that these latter agencies were subject to a premovement, quite different in kind from any which influenced the former ; and this presumption would be very greatly increased by the discoveries of Galileo and his successors. Now it is most remarkable, and bears thinking of again and again, that the only power of indefinite prediction which science has ever procured, concerns cosmical phenomena and not earthly. The spontaneous impression made even on the mind of savages (as we have already said) is that the march of cosmical phenomena is steady and equable, while the march of earthly phenomena is variable and incalculable. The effect of science has been only to make this contrast more striking and more unexceptional than it was before.*

Now there is a further opinion, which (to say the least) is theologically probable in a very high degree; and which (if admitted) will throw great light on this contrast between cosmical and earthly phenomena. It is the received doctrine of the schools—it is far the more obvious implication of Scripture— that there are no rational and immortal creatures, excepting only Angels and men. But if this be so, it would seem necessarily to follow that this planet, and no other, is the abode of rational and immortal creatures. Dr. Whewell's work on " the Plurality of Worlds " showed at the very least that physical science interposes no kind of obstacle to this belief; and we will therefore suppose it to be true. But if this proposition be accepted, you see at once how *à priori probable* it is, that God should confine His constant premovement of physical sequences to that particular planet, which is inhabited by immortal beings; by those beings whom His Son has redeemed; by those beings who can plead for temporal blessings in that Son's availing Name.†

---

* See note at the end of this article.

† A very eminent thinker, whose view of all these matters is diametrically opposed to our own, has most kindly given his attention to this article since it has been in type. He here interposes an objection. He admits most fully the contrast between cosmical and earthly phenomena, as regards their respective capability (in the present state of science) of indefinite prediction. But he urges that a cause may most easily be assigned for this contrast, entirely distinct from any supposition of Divine premovement: viz., the fact that cosmical phenomena depend on causes comparatively simpler and fewer, than those which produce earthly phenomena. It is nothing marvellous, he adds, that we can predict the result of causes which are few and simple, but *cannot* predict the result of those which are most numerous and complicated.

Here the first question to be considered is, whether such difference of causal complexity (however great) would in itself *suffice* to account for the contrast, admitted by our opponent,

At the same time we would beg our readers distinctly to observe, that this contrast between cosmical and earthly phenomena is no essential part of our argument. No scientific man in the world will maintain, that science has *proved* any capability of indefinite prediction to exist, in the case of those temporal goods for which a Christian prays. Our argument then—which is irrefragable and complete—may be thus drawn out. The Christian and Catholic religion has its own intrinsic motives of credibility; and such as may really be called peremptory and conclusive. It is a most certain truth of that religion — it is declared so repeatedly in Scripture that it would be absurd even to attempt an enumeration of texts—that the most available of all methods, for averting temporal calamities and for

---

between these two classes of phenomena. On this question, the present writer is wholly incompetent to form an opinion; but we submit it to the careful consideration of Catholic scientific men. For argument's sake, at all events, we will here concede that our opponent is so far in the right.

We frankly confess then that our *positive* argument from physical science, in behalf of Divine premovement, is very far less strong, than it *would* have been had earthly phenomena resembled cosmical in the simplicity of their causation. Indeed, had this been so, their Divine premovement would have been (so to speak) a visible and palpable fact. But then it is not the general law of God's Providence that the truths of religion *shall* be visible and palpable facts; but, on the contrary, that they shall give occasion to the merit of faith. Let it be assumed then, that God does premove earthly phenomena; and let the further very obvious supposition be also made, that he does not desire this premovement to be a visible and palpable fact. On this supposition, He would act just as we maintain that He *has* acted. He would make earthly phenomena to proceed on so complex a chain of causation, that His assiduous premovement of them eludes direct observation.

At last our opponent admits, with characteristic candour, that science in its present stage is unable to *disprove* the hypothesis of Divine premovement; and, as we state in the text, this is absolutely all which our argument requires.

[It may now be added, without impropriety, that this "very eminent thinker" was the late Mr. Stuart Mill.]

obtaining a healthy proportion of temporal goods, is prayer to God.* And it is an immediate inference from this truth, that God is constantly intervening in the course of nature, according to the inscrutable plans of His Providence. On the other hand, modern physical science has added strength to the proof otherwise existing of another and supplementary truth ; viz., that external phenomena (putting aside the case of Miracles, which is afterwards to be considered) proceed uniformly and invariably on fixed laws. There is no inconsistency whatever, nor any approach to inconsistency, between these two truths ; and the only reasonable course therefore is heartily to embrace them both. It is true therefore, on the one hand, that the laws of external nature (with the above-named exception) are strictly invariable ; but it is equally true on the other hand, that those laws are premoved and directed by God at every moment, according to the dictates of His uncontrolled and inscrutable Will. Philosophers who on theory refuse to pray, pursue a course no less simply unreasonable, than any superstitious Christian (if such there were) who should be deterred, by his belief in the efficacy of prayer, from obtaining medical aid for himself and his family.

One final explanation. Our argument, be it ob-

---

* See e. g. 2 Paralip. xvi, 12, 13 :—" Nec [Asa] in infirmitate suà quæsivit Dominum, *sed magis in medicorum arte confisus est:* dormivitque cum patribus suis." Cf. vv. 7–9 :—" In tempore illo venit Hanani propheta ad Asa regem Judæ et dixit ei : 'Quia *habuisti fiduciam in rege Syriæ et non in Domino Deo tuo,* idcirco evasit Syriæ regis exercitus de manu tuâ. Nonne Æthiopes et Libyes multò plures erant quadrigis et equitibus et multitudine nimiâ quos *cùm Domino credidisses* tradidit in manu tuâ ? Oculi enim Domini *præbent fortitudinem* his *qui corde perfecto credunt in Eum.*' "

[It is extremely observable that S. James chooses Elias's prayer for a material result,—drought,—as his especial type of the Christian's prayer for spiritual good : "Pray for each other's salvation, because the just man's assiduous prayer has great efficacy. Elias prayed," &c.—v. 16–18.]

served, by no means requires us to deny any general
uniformity which experience may indicate, in God's
premovement of natural laws. It may be true e.g.,
that He more often sends rain in July than in June;
and that the amount of rain which falls in one year
is not very different from that which falls in another
year. If scientific observation have established these
facts, they are of course true: but, however true,
they present no difficulty whatever to a Catholic or
to any other Christian. Indeed one would expect à
priori much greater regularity of action from the
All-Wise God, than from the human player on a
musical instrument.

Let us now then consider the treatment given by
our three authors, to that part of the general subject
which has occupied us up to this point. Dr. Gilbert
expresses most fairly and most forcibly, without one
particle of exaggeration, the objection to which we
have been hitherto replying.

Many of you may no doubt also remember, how the futility,
the uselessness of prayer is reported to have been pithily put by
Lord Palmerston, in answer to the deputation which waited upon
him for a public fast-day against the cholera. His answer is said
to have been, "Never mind the fast-day, but cleanse your drains."

From the positions taken by these men and their adherents, it
follows not only that prayer against the cholera is useless, but
that all prayer, where the laws of nature are concerned, is absurd,
useless, puerile, if not positively wicked; so that, if you naturally
suffer from indigestion, a thousand graces before meals will not
save you from the consequences; if you naturally suffer from
sleepless nights, *all the prayers of your friends will not procure as
much sleep as a single drop of laudanum;* the prayer or the blessing of a parent on a child that is leaving his home, perhaps for
ever, avails no more than the rustling of the wind; the prayers
of a whole nation suffering from famine or pestilence affect God
no more than the sorrowful sounds of the wild waves beating
against the hard rocks; and finally, *as all temptations are mostly
dependent upon an unequal distribution of the humours of the body,
a night of prayer will not remove or even lessen one of them.*

With the efficacy of prayer [adds Dr. Gilbert] *the Bible stands
or falls.* Hence the vast importance of the subject; it concerns
not only the members of the one religion, but all who wish to be
Christians, all who hold the Bible to be God's sacred Word (p. 4).

And further—

Besides the testimony of the Bible and Christianity, the instincts of our nature, no matter what our religion may be, proclaim the efficacy of prayer (p. 10).

His own reply to the objection consists of three different particulars. Firstly, he adopts to some extent our own solution—the Divine premovement of natural laws. If *man*, he argues, can modify the laws of nature, how far more readily can this be done by God, the Author of those laws!

How countless are the modifications in natural causes produced by man! You cannot speak, you cannot walk, you cannot light a fire, without such modifications. There is not a word that passes from our lips that does not cause waves and pulsations of the air,—there is not a keel that ploughs the surface of the sea that does not send an influence through the surrounding waters,—there is not a man or beast that treads upon the earth that does not impart a motion to some of the particles thereof, and so modify the power or force of some of the waves of the air and of the sea, and of some of the particles of the land.

Now, as man is continually modifying natural causes, and is thereby curing disease, increasing the fertility of the land and lessening accidents by land and sea;—*allow God a similar power*, and though the laws of nature are immutable, every ordinary prayer can be heard (pp. 14, 15).

Our only comment, so far, would be, that he represents God's " modification of natural causes " as comparatively rare and exceptional; whereas to us it seems far more simple and straightforward, to regard such intervention as unceasing. Such a view seems to us more accordant than any other with the language of theology and Scripture; which surely represent God, not as occasionally interfering, but rather as ruling the events of each successive moment by His inscrutable and uncontrolled Will.

Secondly, Dr. Gilbert suggests (p. 16) that God may really disturb phenomenal uniformity, not in the way of what are commonly called Miracles, but by altering the agency of " second causes out of sight." Such a course of Providence is undoubtedly possible in itself; and we believe we may safely defy scientific men to prove that God never adopts it. At the same time we do not ourselves see any necessity for the supposition, or any evidence of its truth.

But Dr. Gilbert's third suggestion shows, we think, that he has not fully mastered his opponent's view. He says that God may indirectly influence *matter*, by directly influencing *mind*.

. . Could not God, on a similar principle, suppress in man the feelings of anger, jealousy, and revenge, and every temptation? Could He not influence the mind of man, and so prevent him entering on a course of action which would bring ruin on himself and others? Could not God influence the mind of a captain so that he shall perceive a leakage in his vessel, or the mind of an engine-driver and he shall discover an impediment on the line of rails, and such influence shall save themselves and others from mutilation and even death? Could not God influence the mind of a physician, and, when he has ineffectually battled with some disease, suggest some combination of natural remedies which shall meet the peculiarities of the case? And so in numerous instances (p. 15).

Dr. Gilbert is answering certain arguments, which purport to establish the impossibility of God's free and unfettered action on matter. But the very same arguments, if they had any weight at all, would be in every respect equally conclusive against the possibility of His exercising such influence on *mind*. Of course we most fully agree with Dr. Gilbert, that in both cases God does possess this power. We only say that our author cannot logically *assume* God's possession of this power over the mind, as a means of *explaining* how He may possess it over matter.

As to the Duke of Argyll, it is one singular instance of the strange incompleteness with which he has written, that we have found it impossible to decide with certainty whether he does or does not accept our doctrine of Divine premovement. He speaks, e.g., of a " Supreme Will " " moving the hidden springs of nature " (p. 23); of a " Higher

Will moving phenomena" (ib.). He holds (p. 24) that Nature is a " plastic medium through which a Higher Voice and Will *are ever addressing us*." And all this seems directly available towards solving that difficulty, which (as we have already pointed out) he so forcibly and clearly states ; the difficulty alleged against all belief in the efficacy of prayer. And yet it would appear that after all he does *not* make use of these considerations in answer to that difficulty ; but, on the contrary, confines them to the particular case of *miraculous* intervention. He applies them in fact exclusively in that case, to which (as we shall presently contend) they are entirely inapplicable.

Mr. M'Coll, so far as we are able to understand his argument, embraces the precise view which we have ourselves maintained. "Christianity," he says, " teaches the doctrine" "that God is behind the veil of Nature *working always*" (p. 429). But his argument, we think, required that he should have developed this view far more clearly and systematically than he has in fact done.

We have now then answered the first of those objections which we stated at the outset. In reply to the second, nothing more is needed than that we should transfer our argument from the macrocosm to the microcosm ; from the realms of matter to the realms of mind. In this part of our reasoning we may fully admit, for argument's sake, that psychology is a science, in the very same full and unreserved sense in which mechanics and chemistry are such ; that mental phenomena, no less than mechanical and chemical, succeed each other by a sequence which is absolutely fixed and invariable. The uniformity however of *material* phenomena is fully reconcilable with the doctrine of an unintermitting Divine premovement ; and the same truth holds no less clearly in the case of *mental* phenomena also. Nor again does mental science, at all more than mechanical or

chemical, afford the slightest indication, that there exists that *abstract* scientific *possibility of indefinite prediction*, which would alone disprove our doctrine. But now what is Divine Grace—so far as it is contemplated by the action before us—except simply a Divine premovement of mental phenomena ? *
And if we may laudably and efficaciously pray for material benefits,—with far more laudableness and efficacy may we pray for the priceless blessing of richer and more effectual Grace.

No one of our three authors has put forth a reply to this second objection; and Dr. Gilbert indeed, as we have already observed, does not seem aware of its existence.

We are next to enter on Free Will: a far more anxious subject than those hitherto considered, as being so intimately connected with some of the most arduous and mysterious doctrines in Theology. We shall confine ourselves however strictly, to what is absolutely necessary for a due appreciation of the objection which we are to encounter.

The Church allows considerable latitude of opinion on the philosophical questions which concern Free Will. At the same time she fully permits her children to hold—what for ourselves (i. e. the present writer) we do hold—viz., that no view of Free Will is altogether satisfactory to the intellect, except that taken by the Jesuit theologians. These great thinkers—whether they embrace what is commonly called the Molinistic or the Congruistic system, whether they follow Lessius or Suarez,—agree with each other in their definition of liberty. " Potentia libera est quæ, positis omnibus requisitis ad agendum, potest agere et non agere." To appreciate this definition, let us

---

* The office of Grace, in *supernaturalizing* the soul and human action, is of course wholly external to the objection which we are here considering.

consider any given moment of human action. My
soul possesses certain qualities, intrinsic and inherent; certain faculties, tendencies, habits, and
the like: and it is solicited by various motives,
having respectively their own special character, intensity, and direction. In order that my will may
act, nothing more is necessary than that which now
exists: "posita sunt omnia requisita ad agendum."
My will cannot be considered *free*, say these theologians, unless at this very moment it has a real
power, at least of either acting or abstaining from
action. They consider, of course, that in the vast
majority of cases it has *more* power than this; it
has the power of acting with greater or less efficacy
in this or that direction: but unless it have at
least *so much* power as above described, it is not free
at all.

We think that the least valuable part of the Duke
of Argyll's work is that concerned with Free Will.
He professes (p. 337) to oppose Mr. Stuart Mill,
and to expose "a deceptive ambiguity" under which
that philosopher's "doctrine seeks shelter"; but in
fact, to our mind, it is Mr. Mill who is clear-headed,
and the Duke who is misty and confused. His own
view is precisely identical with Mr. Mill's; and it is
strange that he can have entertained any different
notion. "The will of *the lower animals*," he says
frankly (p. 331), "is *as free as ours.* . . . The only
difference is that the will of the lower animals is
acted upon by fewer and simpler motives." "Where
all the conditions of mental action are constant, the
resulting action will be constant too" (p. 338). "*If*
we knew *all* the motives which are brought by external things to bear upon his mind; and *if* we knew
all the other motives which that mind evolves out of
its own powers, and out of previously acquired materials, to bear upon itself; and *if* we knew the constitution of that mind perfectly; . . *then* we should
be able to" calculate "*with certainty* the resulting

course of conduct " (p. 339).* Now there is nothing
to surprise one in the fact that the Duke of Argyll
should hold that deterministic doctrine, which is
embraced by many powerful minds. But surely he
displays much shallowness or thoughtlessness, when
he says (p. 338) that his own view " is not only true,
but something *very like a truism.*" We maintain that,
on the contrary, it is directly subversive, not of Catholicity only but of Natural Religion. Before arguing
however for this proposition, we must make the
reader more clearly understand what is the Duke's
doctrine.

The view advocated then, by Mr. Mill clearly, and
by the Duke obscurely, is this : that in every single
case the will's action is *abstractedly calculable.* Take
an illustration from mechanics. A certain physical
particle, possessing certain intrinsic qualities, is
solicited at this moment by certain attracting forces.
It is admitted by every one, that the movement
immediately resulting is abstractedly calculable. In
other words, any being who should possess adequate
intelligence and infallible accuracy of thought,—who
should know with perfect precision the particle's
intrinsic qualities,—who should know with equal

---

* The Duke's text runs : " If we knew the constitution of the
mind so *perfectly as to estimate exactly the weight it will allow to
all the different motives operating on it.*" We have omitted these
words in the text, as they might tend to distract attention from
the Duke's meaning. They involve a petitio principii ; since
they imply in themselves the deterministic tenet. We precisely
deny of course, that the weight attached to motives *depends* exclusively on " the constitution of the mind." The mind, we
maintain, whatever its constitution, has a certain power of decid-
ing *for itself* what weight it shall attach to motives.

We have also placed the word " calculate " where the Duke
says " predict." The meaning remains exactly the same. But we
think it of great importance, for the sake of clearness, to preserve
a broad verbal distinction, between that " abstract possibility of
indefinite *prediction,*" on which we laid so much stress a few
pages ago ; and that abstract power of immediate *calculation,*
with which alone we are here concerned.

precision the nature, the direction, the intensity, of the soliciting forces,—could calculate with infallible certainty the movement immediately resulting. In like manner, say Mr. Mill and the Duke, let us suppose the mind of any given individual solicited at this moment by certain given motives. "Any being " who should possess adequate intelligence and in- " fallible accuracy of thought,—who should know " with perfect precision that mind's intrinsic and " inherent qualities,—who should know with equal " precision the nature, the direction, the intensity, " of the soliciting motives,—could calculate with " infallible accuracy the movement of will thence " immediately resulting. Or (putting the same thing " briefly) the will's movement at any moment is in " the abstract capable of infallible calculation."

Now we on our side maintain that this tenet is subversive of that doctrine, concerning man's probation by means of Free Will,* which is at the very root not of Catholicity only but of Natural Religion. At this moment I am solicited by various motives; and it is my *probation* of this moment, how I shall comport myself under that solicitation. If I exert myself to please God better, my probation so far is advancing favourably; if otherwise, the reverse. But the very notion of my being on probation *at all*, implies that my will's action cannot be calculated

---

* We purposely avoid saying that the Duke's tenet is inconsistent with the doctrine of Free Will in every imaginable shape, for the following reasons. Jesus and Mary, when on earth, were truly endowed with Free Will : and yet Jesus and Mary—our Lord because He was God, and His Mother because of her singular grace,—always elicited with infallible certainty that movement, which was simply accordant with the Divine Preference. So far therefore as they were concerned, the course of their will at any moment was abstractedly capable of infallible calculation. But then they were *not* on their probation. In like manner, we are not here concerned with the Free will of Beati in Heaven, or of souls in Purgatory.

beforehand; it implies that more than one course is, in the fullest and most unreserved sense, open to my free and unfettered choice. Let me once be persuaded,—not speculatively alone, but practically and energetically,—that my will's action at last can be no less infallibly calculated than the motion of a particle, I sink down paralyzed: religion becomes a mockery; and my Creator's profession of placing me under probation becomes (may He forgive the blasphemy!) a tyrannical insult. This is really one of those truths, which are so undeniable on the very surface, that their evidence is but obscured by any lengthened production of argument.

Our purpose in the present article, as we have throughout explained, is purely defensive. Indeed, had we entertained any thought of *proving* those high religious truths with which we are occupied, we should have found it swell under our hands to a volume. We have now indeed pointed out, that Free Will is an all-important religious truth; that it is a fundamental doctrine, not of Catholicity only, but of Natural Religion: but to enter upon a philosophical argument in its favour, is entirely beyond our scope. What we have here to do, is merely to answer the *objections* brought against it, by such thinkers as Mr. Mill and the Duke of Argyll.

1. Mr. Mill in several parts of his works lays stress on the following :—"All Theists," he says in effect, " must admit that *God* at least does at each moment " infallibly calculate the will's movement; and they " must admit therefore, that it is in the abstract " *capable* of calculation." The reply to this is so obvious, that we have always wondered how this clear and powerful thinker can have been deluded by so transparent a fallacy. We totally deny of course, that God does *calculate* the will's movement in the case of those under probation: on the contrary, His knowledge of that movement supposes, as its very founda-

tion, the will's *free* exercise in this or that direction.* Nay it is not strictly true to say, that God *foresees* acts at all; because He is external to time.

> " Nothing to Him is present, nothing past,
> But an Eternal Now doth ever last."

2. "There is no certainty," says the Duke (pp. 339, 340), " in the world of physics more absolutely certain, than some certainties in the world of mind. We know that a humane man will not do a uselessly cruel action ; we know that an honourable man will not do a base action." Well, there is a multitude of actions so cruel, and another multitude so base, that we may infallibly calculate of a humane and of an honourable man respectively, that he will not (until his character change) commit them. But such a statement has no value as grave reasoning. "Dolus latet in generalibus ": let us take a concrete case. I am a man, we will say, of really humane character. I am sitting comfortably at my fireside on a cold winter's day, with " the Last Chronicle of Barset " in my hands. Suddenly the news reaches me that a friend of mine has been immersed, while skating on a deep pond close to the house. You may calculate no doubt with infallible certainty, that I shall throw down my book and rush to the rescue. But take some case of an immeasurably more frequent kind. I have been in the habit of reading to a poor cripple in the neighbourhood, who has nothing else to cheer him. The last two days I have been unavoidably prevented from going ; and to-day also, if I do not start at once, I shall have no other opportunity. On the other hand, the outside air is cold; while the

---

* " Dei præscientia, ex doctrinâ Patrum, res *liberè* futuras *supponit.*" " In hypothesi quòd res futuræ sint, eo ipso quòd *futuræ sint,* Deus eas videre debet : *consequentur,* nempe, ad *liberam* determinationem . . . Cùm verum sit hominem se determinaturum ad talem vel talem actionem, *hoc ipso* Divinæ notitiæ subest."—*Perrone de Deo,* nn. 393, 400.

fire is warm, and Mr. Trollope (even for him) unusually amusing. Humanity draws me in one
direction, comfort and amusement very strongly in
another. Humanity solicits me to spend an hour in
a cold draughty cottage, occupied in a very dull
employment; comfort and amusement importune me
to stay where I am. Under such circumstances it
is the Duke of Argyll's proposition, that the course
which I shall adopt is as infallibly calculable, as is
the course of a physical particle solicited by diver-
gent forces. Now at all events to allege—as the
Duke alleges—that this proposition is *self-evident*,
is a most startling paradox; a simple outrage on
common sense : you can hardly exaggerate the violent absurdity of so speaking. But we should like
uncommonly to know what possible ground the Duke
has for alleging—we will not say that his proposition
is *self-evident*,—but that it is *true*. For ourselves,
we take the liberty of affirming that it is entirely
false ; and we affirm this of it, because it is peremptorily condemned by religion and morality.

Now it is precisely such cases as these, which are
of every-day occurrence, and on which man's probation mainly turns. The ordinary exhortation of a
priest, or (for that matter) of any religious minister
who is not a Lutheran or a Calvinist, would be, we
strenuously maintain, the only one consistent with
sound philosophy. He would tell me that it is just
on such an issue as this, that my upward or down-
ward course might depend. If I choose the lower
course, he will add,—the course which I well know
to be the less pleasing to my Creator,—I begin the
habit of fully deliberate imperfection ; and on my
next occasion of trial I shall find greater difficulty
than at present, in freely making the better choice.
Let me continue so acting for months and years, I
shall be an immeasurably less humane man at the
end of them than I am at present. On the other
hand, if I correspond with grace and on every such

occasion freely choose the better alternative, then, in the way even of natural consequence, my character will steadily rise ; not to speak of the special benediction which I shall call down on myself, from my loving and approving God. Between these two alternatives, he will continue, I have now and on every such occasion the freest power of choosing. Such are the doctrines which a priest would practically impress on me as speculative truths. They belong to the very alphabet of Natural Religion, but they are doctrines which the Duke of Argyll by implication denies.

The sum then of our reply to this particular argument of the Duke's is simply this. Take any given man at any given moment. There are certain things so good, and certain things so bad, that we may infallibly calculate he will do neither the one nor the other. But then there is a large number of intermediate things, on which no such calculation is even abstractedly possible ; and these are the very things on which his probation turns.*

3. Lastly we are to consider that objection to Free Will, which is most closely identified with the direct purpose of our article. " If this doctrine of Free Will " were true, and of probation by *means* of Free Will, " then the course of mental phenomena is not in " itself calculable ; and if not, then psychology is no " science at all. But such a conclusion is so para- " doxical and so obviously false, as of itself to over- " throw that theory from which it legitimately re- " sults." We admit frankly in reply, that psychology is not as strictly scientific, throughout its whole extent, as mechanics or chemistry. But before replying to the objection which will be *founded* on that admission, we must consider how far the ad-

---

* [The Duke of Argyll commented on these remarks in a subsequent edition of his work and a reply to his comment was published in the "Dublin Review" for October, 1868, pp. 55, 56.]

mission itself should extend. In other words, we will now consider *to what extent*, assuming the doctrine of Free Will, psychology fails of a strictly scientific character.

There are three different classes of mental phenomena : cognitions, volitions, emotions. Psychology then is divisible into five sections : the three former treating respectively these three classes in themselves, and the two latter treating them in their mutual relations. Of these five sections, the four former are absolutely unaffected by the doctrine of Free Will; and are therefore as strictly scientific as mechanics and chemistry. That section of psychology with which alone we are concerned, is that which treats the relation between cognitions and volitions ; between intellect and will. Even as regards this section of psychology, we need only look at one particular sub-section ; viz., the theory of motives. Undoubtedly, granting Free Will, there can be no strictly scientiffc theory of motives. We are now therefore to inquire, how far this particular sub-section of psychology—the theory of motives—is deflected by the doctrine of Free Will from the rigorous character of a science.

We will here then lay down a proposition, which, beyond all possible question, is fully consistent with the doctrine of Free Will; and which for our part we confidently embrace as true. My soul at some given moment possesses certain qualities intrinsic and inherent; certain faculties, tendencies, habits, and the like. It is solicited moreover by certain motives, having their own special character, intensity, and direction. Our proposition is this. Under such circumstances; science (considered in its abstract perfection) may calculate infallibly the " spontaneous resultant " of those motives ; or, in other words, my will's " spontaneous impulse." Now this proposition is indubitably consistent with Free Will; because I have the fullest power of *opposing* my will's spon-

tancous impulse. My thoughts are at this moment
perhaps predominantly influenced by worldly or
sensual motives. I may turn them however by an
effort towards what is heavenly and divine; but if I
do *not* put forth some exertion, I follow as a matter
of course my will's spontaneous impulse. How far
I may *choose* to put forth such exertion,—*this* is not
abstractedly matter of calculation at all. I acquit
myself more laudably under my probation, precisely
in proportion as I more frequently and more energetically put forth effort in a good direction.* At
the same time it should be observed, that in all
ordinary cases the act of will, which results *in fact*,
is found in *close vicinity* to the will's spontaneous
impulse. It is only in the rarest and most exceptional cases,—or, rather (we may say) it never
happens at all,—that a man of ordinary piety will
be found putting forth an act of heroic saintliness.
In 999 cases out of 1,000 a man's probation is
carried to a successful issue, by this more than by
anything else; viz., by putting forward on repeated
occasions a number of acts, which are *a little* higher
than his spontaneous impulse. Nor does any exception to this general remark strike us at the moment,
except those cases in which there is a violent temptation to mortal sin.

We maintain then, that so far as regards, not the
will's *actual movement* but its *spontaneous impulse*,
there is a theory of motives as strictly scientific, as
abstractedly capable of scientific calculation, as any
theory of mechanics or chemistry. But we further
maintain that, in applying that theory to practice,
allowance must always be made for the fact, that in
every instance the will has a real power of acting

---

* The whole doctrine of preventing and assisting grace is of
course *in fact* most intimately bound up with all this; but our
argument against Determinism may be conducted legitimately,
without encumbering it with this further question.

above the level of such spontaneous impulse. How far the will may *choose* to do so, is a matter incapable of calculation, and external to science altogether. And this circumstance precisely, neither more nor less, constitutes that one particular, in which the doctrine of Free Will interferes with the strictly scientific character of psychology.

We are next then to inquire, what arguments our opponents can adduce, for the purpose of showing that psychology has a more unreservedly scientific character than we have here assigned to it. Now there are certain German writers, we believe, who have maintained that the fact of phenomenal uniformity can be established on purely à priori grounds; indeed, that it is not a mere *fact* at all, but as necessary a *truth* as the very axioms and theorems of geometry. We are wholly unaware however of the grounds on which they base so strange an assertion; nor do we know in what direction to look for those grounds.

But the writers with whom we are immediately concerned, do not dream of putting forth any such peremptory pretension. We cannot take any more unexceptionable specimen of them than Mr. Mill; nor again can anything be more intelligible and simple than the position which he takes up. (See his Logic, bk. iii. c. 3, and c. 21.) Scientific men, he says, ground their belief of phenomenal uniformity exclusively on their *observation* of that uniformity. Consequently, "the uniformity in the succession of events," and generally of phenomena, " must be received, *not as a law of the universe*, but of that portion of it only which is within the range of *our means of sure observation*." (Conclusion of c. 21.)

The present issue then is reduced to one, which would appear very narrow and very easily decided. Can Mr. Mill, or any one else, allege any observed facts, which vindicate for mental phenomena any greater uniformity of sequence than we have above assigned to them? Neither on Mr. Mill's part, nor on the Duke of Argyll's, have we observed the slightest *attempt* to adduce such facts. The doctrine of Free Will rests on philosophical arguments, which we do not profess here to adduce, but than which no stronger (as we confidently think) ever established a philosophical conclusion. We verily believe that in no other case has so strongly-demonstrated a doctrine been opposed so confidently, we had almost said so superciliously, on grounds so frivolous, poverty-stricken, and meagre.

Take, for instance, Mr. Mill, a thinker of real genius and depth. With the single exception of that weak piece of reasoning above quoted, based on God's foreknowledge of human action, we are really not aware of one single argument, good, bad, or indifferent, which he has ever brought against the doctrine of Free Will.* He commonly contents himself with stating repeatedly and emphatically the *contradictory* tenet, that all mental phenomena proceed on an absolutely fixed and invariable sequence. He constantly speaks of this tenet, as though it were self-evident; and as though it sufficed therefore, *by* such self-evidence, to disprove the dogma of Free Will. The Duke of Argyll indeed has adduced two reasons for the deterministic view; but they appear to us singularly feeble. One has been already noticed above : the other is rather implied in various places (see e.g. pp. 352, 363, 366) than directly stated. If the will were free, he says in effect, the science of politics would be impossible; for that science proceeds on an assumption, that you may calculate the effect of this or that motive on the people's mind. We reply very easily. It results from what has been above said, that the

---

* [This was published before the appearance of Mr. Mill's work on Sir W. Hamilton.]

" spontaneous impulse " of man's will under given circumstances, is a matter in itself as simply capable of scientific calculation, as is the motion of a physical point solicited by given attractions. And this truth is an abundantly sufficient basis for political science.

In fact it is obvious, as soon as stated, that you confer on men a moral benefit which no words can exaggerate, by placing them under the best motives ; i.e. by placing them under motives, the " spontaneous resultant " of which shall be morally good in the highest attainable degree. This principle, as we have seen, is most fully consistent with Free Will ; and yet it is all which the politician can possibly need as a motive for action. Nor can any one dream that the Church has been blind or indifferent to this principle, who considers the unparalleled stress which she has ever laid e.g. on a good education : on the contrary it may rather be affirmed, that there is no philosophical doctrine in the world which has had so large an influence on her whole practical conduct. All that can be said on the other side is, that she has not exhibited that narrowness of thought which in this respect characterizes certain anti-Catholic philosophers. For, in remembering the unspeakable importance of good motives, she has not forgotten what may be called the opposite pole of sound doctrine ; viz., the will's real power of choice, and God's probation of man by means of that power.

The objection, which remains to be considered, concerns *Miracles*. Certainly, if the question of Miracles were to be discussed in its full extent, it would require an article to itself ; but the mere answer to this particular objection may be given very briefly and easily. The objection, our readers may remember, is this :—" To assert the past or " present existence of miracles, is to deny that the

" laws of nature are absolutely fixed; and to deny
" this, is to deny the very possibility of physical
" science." We admit the former of these two
propositions, but deny the latter. We say that the
interest of physical science is in no respect affected
by the existence of miracles, because *these are
always accompanied by visible symbols of Divine intervention.* And now to explain our meaning in this
reply.

We cannot do better than repeat the argument
which, at starting, we put into the mouth of our
imaginary objector. "I compose a substance to-
" day of certain materials, and find it, by experi-
" ment, to be combustible: I compose another to-
" morrow, of the very same materials, united in the
" very same way, and the very same proportions;
" and I find the composition *in*combustible. If
" such a case were possible, the whole foundation
" of science would be taken from under my feet."
This allegation we consider incontrovertible; but
then this is *not* the case of a *miracle.* Let us then
vary our supposition. On the second occasion, when
I enter my laboratory to make the desired experiment, I find a venerable man seated. He announces
himself as commissioned by God to deliver me some
authoritative message. "And now," he adds, "I
will give you a proof that He sent me. You know,
by experiment, that the substance in your hand is
naturally combustible; but now place it in the same
fire, or in one a thousand times fiercer, and it shall
remain unscathed." If I find the fact to be so, I
shall indeed have extremely strong ground for believing my visitor Divinely commissioned; but I
shall have no ground whatever for doubting that
the substance is naturally combustible. Nay, my
conviction of this fact will be even strengthened.
For my visitor assumed that it was *naturally* combustible, by the very fact of treating its non-com-
bustion as a *miracle.*

And the same answer may be made, however numerous may be the miracles wrought. The infidel Gibbon, when speaking of " the innumerable prodigies which were performed in Africa by the relics of S. Stephen," has this most shallow remark. " A miracle," he says, " in that age of superstition and credulity, lost *its name* and its merit, since it would scarcely be considered as a deviation from *the ordinary and established laws of nature.*" Now let us even make the wild and extravagant supposition, that some given law of nature, in some given time and place, were far more frequently suspended by miracle, than allowed to take its natural course. Let us imagine e.g., that England were again Catholic ; and that every Englishman, by invoking S. Thomas of Canterbury, could put his hand into the fire without injury. Why the very fact that in order to avoid injury he must invoke the Saint's name, would ever keep fresh and firm in his mind the conviction, that fire does naturally burn. He would therefore as unquestioningly, in all his physical researches, assume this to *be* the natural property of fire, as though God had never wrought a miracle at all.

The Duke of Argyll says (p. 89, note), that " the question of Miracles seems now to be admitted *on all hands* to be simply a question of evidence." We are extremely glad that the Duke can credit this ; and we should be still more rejoiced if we could entirely credit it ourselves. For saying precisely this, Father Newman a few years back was assailed most violently, not by infidels and semi-infidels only, but by High-Church Anglicans ; by the " Guardian " newspaper. However, *many* thinkers of the day must really admit this, or else the Duke could not possibly have thought that *all* admit it ; and he quotes no less an authority than Professor Huxley, as counting it " unjustifiable " to " deny the possibility of miracles." The question of evidence then assumes singular importance; and we hope that both the Duke and the Professor will carefully study the evidence on which approved Catholic miracles rest. Dr. Gilbert has done great service by bringing this before the notice of Protestants.

Four miracles are required to be proved for beatification, and two more for canonization; and these must be proved *by eye-* and *not by car-witnesses.*

In miracles where diseases have been cured, it is required : (1) that the disease must be of an aggravated nature, and difficult or impossible to be cured ; (2) that it was not on the turn ; (3) that no medicine had been used, or, if it had, that it had done no good; (4) the cure must be sudden ; (5) the cure must be perfect ; (6) there must have been no crisis. Could there be greater caution ?

In the process of investigation no step is taken, no doubt propounded, without many of the members being present, and a printed report of each session being sent to those who are absent. Besides the cross-examinations, which are of a most scrutinising character, it is the sole duty of one of the leading members, the Promoter Fidei, to make objections and, if possible, to disprove every reported miracle.

In cases of epilepsy thirteen years are required to elapse before miracles are approved, for fear of a relapse ; in cases of hydrophobia and nervous diseases a longer period is necessary : whilst the opinions of physicians, surgeons, scientific men, and eyewitnesses, are taken down in writing.

Let me suppose that the miracle for investigation is the recovery of a person's sight. First of all, it has to be proved whether the person was born blind or became so afterwards ; secondly, the duration of the blindness ; thirdly, the cure in its most minute details ; fourthly, the written opinion of the best scientific and medical men in Italy as to the cause of the blindness ; fifthly, *whether it is possible to refer the miracle to natural causes ;* sixthly, *whether the miracle was instantaneous* . . . . . . and, seventhly, whenever the physicians and scientific men cannot trace the cause of the blindness no decision is ever come to.

Indeed, so sifting and exhausting is the investigation, that Alban Butler tells us, on the authority of Daubenton, that an English Protestant gentleman, being present, and seeing the process of several miracles, said they were incontestable ; but was utterly surprised at the scrupulosity of this scrutiny when told that *not one of those had been allowed by the Congregation of Rites to have been sufficiently proved.*

Perrone also asserts that he showed the process for certain

miracles to a Protestant lawyer of some eminence, who was perfectly satisfied with the testimony and the reasoning, and declared that they ought to stand before any English jury; but was astonished when he was assured that the evidence was *not considered sufficient by the Congregation of Rites* (pp. 49–50).

It may be well also to quote a passage written by F. Newman, in the course of that discussion to which we have already referred; because it is precisely to the question of *evidence* that he directs his remarks :—

Putting out of the question the hypothesis of unknown laws of nature (which is an evasion from the force of any proof), I think it impossible to withstand the evidence which is brought for the liquefaction of the blood of S. Januarius at Naples, and for the motion of the eyes of the pictures of the Madonna in the Roman States. I see no reason to doubt the material of the Lombard crown at Monza; and I do not see why the Holy Coat at Trèves may not have been what it professes to be. I firmly believe that portions of the True Cross are at Rome and elsewhere; that the Crib of Bethlehem is at Rome; and the bodies of S. Peter and S. Paul also. I believe that at Rome, too, lies S. Stephen; that S. Matthew lies at Salermo, and S. Andrew at Amalfi. I firmly believe that *the relics of the Saints are doing innumerable miracles and graces daily;* and that it needs only for a Catholic to show devotion to any Saint in order to receive special benefits from his intercession. I firmly believe that Saints in their lifetime have before now *raised the dead to life, crossed the sea without vessels, multiplied grain and bread, cured incurable diseases,* and stopped the operation of the laws of the universe in a multitude of ways. ("Lectures on Catholicism in England.")

Here then we bring to a close our treatment of that question, which we began by raising. It must not be forgotten however, that the Church teaches not a Divine only, but also a diabolical, intervention in phenomena. Within certain limits fixed by God, evil spirits are permitted on the one hand, to premove the laws of nature; on the other hand, to violate those laws by certain portents, which in some sense simulate the character of Divine miracles. It is evidently impossible, without an intolerable lengthiness, here to enter on this important field of inquiry; but the preceding remarks will suffice to show the general view of it; which we should be disposed to take.

We said at starting that we could only attempt to state, in the merest skeleton outline, that reply which (as it seems to us) may be most conclusively given to one whole class of objections against religion ; and that too a class immeasurably more specious and formidable, than any other of those derived from experimental science. This class is more specious than any other, because the very foundation of experimental science is phenomenal uniformity ; and because phenomenal uniformity seems on the surface directly contradictory to the Catholic doctrine on Prayer, on Grace, on Free Will, and on Miracles. As to the principles we have put forth in defence of this doctrine, we would say to any reader who is versed at once in theological and in experimental science,

Si quid novisti rectius istis,
Candidus imperti ; si non, his utere mecum.

Nor are we without hope that some one, competent to the task, may complete them where they are defective ; may expand them into fulness ; may carry them out into detail ; and may illustrate them with a number of relevant scientific facts.

To conclude. Catholics and Christians generally are much too cowardly, we think, in presence of the so-called scientific world ; and give far more weight to its view of things, than is at all deserved. Scientific men exhibit a confidence, peremptoriness, sometimes superciliousness, which gives an impression of their having far more of argument at their back than really exists.* We should run counter

---

* "Nothing is more common," says the Duke of Argyll most truly (p. 113), "than to find men who may be trusted thoroughly on the facts of their own science, but who *cannot be trusted for a moment on the place which these facts assume in the general system of truth.* Philosophy must include science ; but science does not necessarily include philosophy."

indeed to the Church's whole teaching, if we sought to repel them by denying either the truth or the value of experimental science; but we ought most carefully to distinguish between the *genuine* principles of such science, and others which so many of its votaries most gratuitously assume. Never perhaps was it so important as it is now, to set forth the Church's rightful claim of authority over the whole field of secular science, so far as the latter directly or indirectly touches the truths of religion. Let Catholics make the Church's doctrine their one centre of thought; and let them so arrange the lessons of science, that in due subordination these may cluster around that centre. Studied on any other principle, secular science can only issue in mischief and deceit; it will be an ignis fatuus, and no true guiding light.

Nor again, in our humble judgment, do Catholics act wisely, who think of delaying their offensive measures against the enemy, until science shall have directly and expressly attacked religion; for by that time the evil will have got to a far more unmanageable head.* No: let them be prompt in assailing and exposing every irreligious principle which scientific men may assume, even though these latter are employing it principally or even exclusively in their own special and immediate sphere. False and evil principles have their own legitimate issue, and are ever most assuredly tending to that issue: whatever may be the present intention of this or that individual, who is unhappily their slave and victim.

ORIGINAL NOTE OF APRIL, 1867.—After this article had gone to press, we lighted by the merest accident

---

* [This was written in 1867. Certainly at this moment "science has attacked religion" with abundant "directness" and "expressness."]

on the following letter from Professor Mansel to
Dr. Pusey, quoted by the latter in his sermon on
" The Miracles of Prayer," pp. 33-35. Its coinci-
dence with what we have said in pp. 26-34 is somewhat remarkable ; because the present writer's view
has been very long in his mind, and belongs to a far
earlier date than Professor Mansel's letter :—

DEAR DR. PUSEY,—The following is a very rough statement of
the matter on which I spoke to you this morning. I have not had
time to think it over carefully, and I am by no means confident
that my view will stand a critical examination.

The assumption that the existence of fixed laws of nature is
incompatible with the intervention of special acts of God's Providence, and that science, in so far as it establishes the former,
tends to overthrow our belief in the latter, appears to me to rest
on a confusion between two very different kinds of natural law.

There are some sciences, such as astronomy, whose laws are to a
great extent expressed in the form of statements of the *periodical
recurrence* of certain phænomena. But there are other sciences,
having also their fixed laws, in which the laws involve no statement of *time*. Thus it is a law of optics that, for the same
medium, the sines of the angles of incidence and refraction are in
an invariable ratio to each other ; and it is a law of chemistry
that elements combine in definite proportions ; but these laws say
nothing about the *time* when any given refraction or combination
will take place.

Now it is reasonable to infer, when a science has accumulated a
certain number of laws of a given kind, that further progress in
the science will discover more laws of the same kind : e.g., that
when astronomy has discovered regular periods for the orbits of
planets, similar discoveries may be made for comets ; but it is
illogical to go per saltum from one science to another, unless the
laws already discovered in the latter science are of the same kind
with those of the former. Chemistry or optics might be advanced
by the discovery of new laws similar to the above, without any
approach to a fixing of the time of phænomena such as exists in
astronomy. It is even conceivable that the progress of a science
might disturb the regularity of occurrence. If men were to
acquire vast powers of producing atmospheric phænomena, the
periodical recurrence of such phænomena would become more
irregular, being producible at the will of this or that man. There
is a remarkable note in Darwin's " Botanic Garden " (canto iv.,
l. 320), in which the author conjectures that changes of wind may
depend on some minute chemical cause, which, if it were discovered, might probably, like other chemical causes, be governed
by human agency. Whatever may be thought of the probability

of this anticipation being realized, it is at least sufficient to suggest one reflection. If atmospheric changes may conceivably, without any violation of natural law, be brought under the control of man, *may they not now, equally without violation of natural law, be under the control of God?* And are we so fully informed of the manner of God's working with regard to this contingent phænomena of nature, as to know for certain that He can never exercise such a control for purposes connected with His moral government?

Is, then, our knowledge of the external conditions, say of health or disease, *likely to make a progress analogous to that of astronomy, or to that of chemistry?* We may discover that certain conditions of the atmosphere are regularly followed by certain states of health, as that certain chemical elements will produce certain results; but we do not thereby discover that those conditions must take place at a given time. Unless we have evidence that the law which manifests God's Will is a law of *periodical recurrence*, as in the case of the sun's rising, there is no more incongruity in praying for the removal of a pestilence than in asking a chemist to perform a particular operation. *We do not ask the chemist to violate the laws of chemistry, but to produce a particular result in accordance with those laws. Do we necessarily do more than this when we pray that God will remove from us a disease?*

If some changes of weather, or of health, had already become matter of certain prediction, like eclipses, we might reasonably presume that others would hereafter become equally certain. If we knew for certain the periodic times of fever, we might hereafter discover those of cholera; if we could now predict how many showers of rain will fall in the course of the present year, we might hereafter be able to make a similar prediction as regards thunderstorms. But has the progress of science in these matters hitherto been of *this kind?* If not, may not science advance indefinitely without in any way interfering with the duty of prayer? And has not the progress of the majority of sciences actually been of this kind?

Believe me yours very truly,
H. L. MANSEL.

Some of Dr. Pusey's own remarks also are well worth quoting :—

I may say freely that I do not see that anything more has been discovered, than certain proximate causes and effects, or some large physical laws, which, although they minister in their different ways to our well-being, yet, in their incalculable compass of variation, do not in the least account for those changes that most affect us. Thus, believing, as scientific men inform us, that the average quantity of rain, which falls in the year in a given place, does not much vary, and that the winds, from the different quarters, in each year blow in much the same proportions; yet they are not these general laws, which affect those things, upon which plenty or famine, health or disease, depend. A concentration of rain or its absence, uninjurious at other times, would ruin seed-time or harvest. Locusts, or perhaps cholera, may be brought at one time by winds which in other parts of the year, or in successive years, might be even beneficial. The growth of spring-corn in our climate depends, we are told, upon a nice adjustment of fine weather and showers. And yet some of us remember a spring when, scarcely any autumn corn having been sown (on account of the wetness of the season, which was continued or renewed in the spring) just at the very last we had exactly that succession of dry weather and rain which was needed. This was one only of several successive seasons in which, at the moment of extreme necessity, God gave us the weather which we needed. And yet they are, most of all, these minute variations, which are, as yet, perfectly unaccountable by science. All the proximate causes and effects of conditions of the atmosphere are no more interrupted, *if, as most of us believe, they are regulated by the immediate Will of God directing and dispensing them,* than the inherent forces, upon whose combination the going of a watch, or the motion of a steam-engine, or the discharge of cannon, depends, are *by the interposition of human will,* regulating those forces so that the watch or the steam-engine should go faster or slower, or the direction of the steam-engine or the range of the cannon should be changed.

THE END.

www.ingramcontent.com/pod-product-compliance
Lightning Source LLC
Chambersburg PA
CBHW030006030726
47499CB00008B/2928

*9 7 8 3 3 3 7 2 7 8 7 8 6 *